The Accomplices

The Accomplices

GEORGES SIMENON

TRANSLATED FROM THE FRENCH BY
BERNARD FRECHTMAN

HAMISH HAMILTON
LONDON

First published in Great Britain, 1966
by Hamish Hamilton Ltd.
*90 Great Russell Street London WC*1

Copyright © 1955 *by Georges Simenon*
Translation Copyright © 1964 *by Georges Simenon*

First published in France 1955
under the title Les Complices

PRINTED IN GREAT BRITAIN BY
WESTERN PRINTING SERVICES LTD, BRISTOL

Chapter One

IT was brutal, instantaneous. And yet he was neither surprised nor resentful, as if he had always been expecting it. He realized in a flash, as soon as the horn started screaming behind him, that the catastrophe was inevitable and that it was his fault.

It was not an ordinary horn that was pursuing him with a kind of anger and terror, but a mournful, agonizing howl such as one hears in a port on a foggy night.

At the same time, he saw in his mirror the red and black bulk of a huge bus bearing down on him and the contracted face of a man with grizzled hair, and he realized that he himself was driving in the middle of the road.

It did not occur to him to free his hand which Edmonde continued to press between her thighs. He would not have had time.

He had almost reached the bottom of the Big Hill where the road took a ninety-degree turn to the right and seemed, from a distance, to be blocked by the wall surrounding the Château Roisin estate.

It had been raining for some minutes, just enough to cover the asphalt with a sticky film.

Oddly enough, at that moment he accepted everything, both the catastrophe and his guilt. He knew that his life was about to be cut in two, that perhaps it was going to be over, and, without believing in what he was doing, he did what had to be done. He made an effort with his free left hand to pull over to the right. But, as he expected, the car skidded and whipped around into a position athwart the road.

Nevertheless, the bus whizzed by miraculously, and Lambert thought he heard the oath that the terrified driver shrieked at him. Behind the glass, he caught sight of the heads of children who were not aware of anything. There was a shock, a tearing of sheet metal, and the mastodon, which had hit a tree, kept rolling, sideways, to the bottom of the slope.

His own car, which had almost stopped, picked up speed again, docilely, as if nothing had happened, whereas the bus crashed headlong with all its mass into the Château Roisin wall.

Lambert did not stop, did not think of stopping. He fled so as not to see and had the presence of mind not to follow the highway but to take the road to the right that led to La Galinière.

Edmonde had not screamed, had not moved. He had merely felt her body stiffen and draw back, and it seemed to him that she had shut her eyes.

He dared not look in the mirror to see what was happening behind him, but he could not help casting a quick glance before the first turn and seeing a blazing mass.

Never had he had such a ghastly sensation in all his being, not even when he had been buried by the bursting of a shell. It seemed impossible that he could keep driving, breathing, looking in front of him. Something was going to crack in his head, or in his chest, and he was in such a sweat that his hands slid on the wheel.

He thought of stopping, of turning around, but he simply couldn't. It was beyond his power. He didn't want to see. Panic drove him forward, an uncontrollable force on which he had no grip.

6

And yet he was able to think of details. At about a hundred yards from the turn, from the wall into which the bus had just crashed, was a petrol station and snack bar run by Despujols and his wife. He knew them. He knew everyone within a radius of five miles from town. Old Madame Despujols was deaf, but her husband, who must have been working in the garden at that hour, had probably heard the crash. Did they have a phone? He couldn't remember. If not, Despujols would have to go to Saint-Marc, a hamlet half a mile away, to give the alarm. He did not have a car. He would go by bicycle.

Lambert still did not dare look at Edmonde, who remained motionless. She must have pulled down her dress without his noticing, for he no longer saw the light colour of her knees.

Something had to be done, he had to go somewhere, he did not yet know where. Now that he had taken the bend and was on the road to La Galinière, he had lost the right to turn round and go back. Nor did he dare show himself in the village, which was half a mile away. He took the first side-road, on the left, frightened at the thought that he might pass a peasant.

If he got to the Coudray highway, he would be safe. He could pretend to be coming from anywhere, not to know anything, not to have been on the Big Hill that day.

A farm loomed up on the right, but he saw no one. It was still raining, a late-summer slanting rain, almost an autumn rain. His heart kept pounding away. His damp hand continued to tremble on the wheel.

He was ashamed, and he felt miserable. Yet he was already forcing himself to think of everything, to foresee, and he heard himself say aloud:

'We'll stop at Tréfoux.'

7

It was almost on the other side of town, around which wound the road to Coudray. He was familiar with all the roads, for he had construction jobs going on all over the region and he inspected the work almost every day. It so happened that he was on his way back from one of the jobs, at the Renondeau farm, where his men were putting up a metal barn.

He was also the builder of the milk co-operative in Tréfoux, which had a model cheese-dairy, and his men were now setting up, two hundred yards from the buildings, a large pig farm which would use the by-products.

He had worked hard, even harder than his father, harder than anyone else in town, and the labour of twenty-five years was now suddenly being threatened.

How many seconds had it taken? So few! Not even time enough for him to remove his right hand.

The driver must have blown his horn the first time about halfway up the hill. He wasn't sure. He hadn't been paying attention. Nevertheless, it came back to him as fragments of a dream come back. The driver had blown his horn to warn him. He had been going fast, driving children from a summer camp back to Paris or some city in the north.

Lambert finally reached the main road, and from then on it was as if he were returning to life. Cars and trucks were speeding along the smooth highway. Three hundred yards away was a red petrol pump, and a little farther on was an inn with a terrace. He almost stopped there for a drink, perhaps to create an alibi by saying casually that he was coming from the Renondeau farm and was on his way to Tréfoux.

Wasn't that being too cautious? Wasn't there a danger of its being used against him? He often stopped at a country bar to drink a half-bottle of white wine, but never when his secretary was with him.

Edmonde seldom accompanied him. He could not have said why he had suddenly said to her this time, as he was about to leave for the farm:

'Take the blueprints with you, Mademoiselle Pampin, and wait for me in the car.'

Marcel, his brother, who was in the office, had looked at him in that calm, exasperating way of his. What could Marcel have been thinking? Everyone lives in his own particular way. Marcel had chosen the life he wanted and seemed content with it. That was no reason for forcing his principles on others.

'Do you need the plans?'

Joseph Lambert had looked his brother in the eyes and answered, 'I do.'

This was not the first time they had affronted each other in that way, if it could be called affronting, since Marcel invariably backed down—which, be it added, is also a manner of speaking, for Marcel merely did not insist but simply looked at his brother with a smile that was as light as his blond, fluffy little moustache.

At that moment, it was not yet raining. The sun flooded the offices, which had been completely remodelled three years before and were separated, as in modern establishments, by glass walls. Joseph alone had an office in which he could isolate himself, in which it was even permissible, under the pretext that the sun was too bright, to lower the Venetian blinds. Therefore, nothing prevented him from calling in Mademoiselle Pampin as if he were going to dictate to her, or for some other work, for nobody, not even Marcel, would have taken the liberty of entering without knocking.

9

What had just happened was no doubt bound to happen. He had said, without thinking, without any precise desire:

'*Take the blueprints with you, Mademoiselle Pampin, and wait for me in the car.*'

She was not unaware of what that meant.

They had driven about a mile south of town when suddenly they heard the fire siren.

Lambert knew it was too late. He had been in the war, he had seen tanks and trucks go up in flames and planes shot down.

He had to keep cool, to ignore the wail of the siren which reminded him of the desperate scream of the bus.

The dairy was lower down, on the bank of the same canal where his own plant was located, but the latter was on the edge of the town, just a stone's throw from a populous neighbourhood. The men who worked on the new pig-farm had just knocked off, and the only one around was the foreman, who was about to leave on his bicycle, carrying the knapsack in which he had brought his lunch. He put his hand to his cap.

'Good evening, Monsieur Joseph.'

He had worked for Lambert senior for more than thirty years and had known his sons when they were youngsters. He called them Monsieur Marcel, Monsieur Joseph. He seldom had occasion to say Monsieur Fernand, since the third brother lived in Paris and hardly ever went back to his home town.

'Good evening, Nicolas. Everything all right?'

Edmonde had not got out of the car. For the first time since the Big Hill, Lambert ventured a glance at her. Would anyone have suspected, from looking at her, that she had just been involved in a catastrophe?

10

She was, of course, pale, but hardly more than usual. Her skin was naturally colourless, which was all the more surprising since she had the round face, full cheeks, and tall body of a healthy girl.

'Did you have time to prepare the girders?'

'A few minutes before the shower. Did you hear the siren? There must have been a fire somewhere.'

'Must have been,' repeated Lambert.

It bothered him to feel that Edmonde was staring at him. What was she thinking? What did she think about what had happened? About what he had done? What was she thinking about him at that very moment? There was no way of telling. Never had he seen a face so indifferent as hers, and her body was as motionless as her features. One could have observed her for minutes on end without seeing a movement.

When he had hired her the year before, after the failure of Penjard, the hardware dealer, whose secretary she had been, the clerks were at first amused by her name and never missed an opportunity to repeat it and dwell on its syllables in a humorous way:

'*Good morning, Mademoiselle Pampin!*'

'*Good-bye, Mademoiselle Pampin!*'

Among themselves they referred to her as *la Pampine*, and one day, through his open window, Lambert had heard a young mason say:

'*That one's all animal!*'

A man wearing corduroy breeches and leather leggings was walking towards them from the dairy, of which he was the manager. Lambert, who was standing near the car, put out his hand and the foreman again touched his cap.

'Hello, Bessières.'

11

'Hello, Monsieur Lambert.'

'Did you hear the sirens?' asked old Nicolas.

'Yes, and I immediately put in a call to town. It seems that a bus full of children crashed into the Château Roisin wall and caught fire.'

He took out his handkerchief and wiped away the beads of sweat on his forehead. He had six children. They were playing in the yard of the dairy. And his wife was pregnant again.

This was the first serious test. Lambert, who had not been expecting it so soon, did not have time to decide what attitude to assume. Edmonde's presence disturbed him. He was surprised to hear himself say, in a natural tone:

'A summer camp?'

'Probably. There are no details.'

Lambert also wiped his face, with what seemed to him a calm movement, and glanced at his hand to see whether it was trembling. It was better not to say that he had come from the Renondeau farm by the Coudray highway. He was always tempted to talk too much.

'I came to take a look,' he murmured. 'Nicolas was telling me that if we have a few sunny days the whole job will be finished by the end of the month.'

'Will you come in and have a drink?'

'Thanks, but I still have work to do at the office.'

He had behaved normally. It had gone off as usual between people who had known each other a long time and had occasion to meet often.

'Is everything all right at home?'

Instead of answering, Bessières muttered, 'I wonder whether I oughtn't to drive out and take a look at what happened over there.'

12

That was all. Lambert got in his car and drove back. In the suburbs and then in town there was already an atmosphere of abnormal excitement. Groups were standing in front of doorways. Men and boys were riding off on their bicycles, all in the same direction.

In the Town Hall Square, where he had an appointment to play bridge at the Café Riche in half an hour, he passed an ambulance, which looked empty, on its way to the hospital. That was the worst moment of all. He almost stopped at the kerb, as if all the energy had drained out of him.

In the café he caught sight of Lescure, the insurance agent, in the company of Nédelec. They were already at their table.

'Aren't you going to stop at the office?' asked Edmonde, as he seemed undecided.

It was the first time she had opened her mouth since the Big Hill. Her tone of voice was indifferent. He nevertheless wondered whether her question was not a discreet reminder.

'Perhaps I ought to.'

'It's half-past six,' she added.

He did not understand what the time had to do with it.

'What of it?'

'I was wondering whether you wanted me to go with you to the Quai Colbert or whether it wouldn't be better for me to get out here.'

She was right. The office closed at half-past six.

'You can get out.'

'Shall I leave the papers with you?'

'Yes, do.'

'Good-bye, Monsieur Lambert.'

'Good-bye, Mademoiselle Pampin.'

13

She shut the door and went off in the direction of the nearby Saint-Georges quarter, where she lived with her mother. On seeing her disappear, he felt both relieved and slightly bewildered. They hadn't agreed on anything. They had made no allusion to what had happened. He didn't know whether she would talk or not. Did he even know what kind of person she was?

'Are you coming?' asked Weisberg, the owner of a local department store, another one of the bridge players, just as Lambert was starting up his engine.

'Not immediately. I've got to drop in at the office.'

'Have you just got into town?'

'This very minute.'

'Have you heard the news?'

'I was told about it at the dairy.'

'I went over to take a look, but I couldn't. It was so awful that I rushed home to make sure my children were alive.'

Lambert managed to ask, 'Was anyone uninjured?'

'No one. To be more exact, one of the girls. There were boys and girls in the bus. But it'll be a miracle if they manage to save her. Benezech is out there. So are the gendarmes. They're expecting the Deputy Prefect any minute, and the Prefect said he'll come before dark.'

Benezech, the local Chief of Police, was another one of the bridge players, a tall red-headed man with a bushy moustache and long light hair on his hands.

'See you later.'

'All right, see you later.'

In an hour, in two hours, perhaps no one would be talking to him in that tone, and perhaps there would be no one left to shake his hand. He had driven off, and all along the road people's faces were more grave and grim than usual. Women were crying on the pavements and in the stores.

As far as he remembered, there had been no traffic on the road when he drove down the Big Hill. He was practically sure that there had been no cars coming in his direction, and he had not seen any truck parked in the middle of the hill, as often happened.

But weren't there any bicycles? Would he have noticed them?

And when he turned right in the direction of La Galinière, wasn't some member of the Despujols family on the doorstep? That was unlikely, but not impossible. His car was black, but there were lots of others like it in town and in the surrounding area. People rarely have the presence of mind to note the number on a licence plate.

A peasant in his field, for example, might very well have recognized him as he drove by. He had a distinctive face, and he was one of the well-known men of the region.

From Château Roisin onwards, he was practically sure of himself, for everything had automatically registered in his memory, including a reddish brown cow that had escaped from its pasture and was wandering along the edge of the road.

But higher up? The man with the goats, in particular, whose name he didn't know, an odd creature who owned a shanty on the main road and who took his four or five nanny goats out to pasture along the road for hours on end?

People were so used to seeing his figure when they drove up or down the Big Hill that they paid no attention to it. At that moment, Lambert did not yet have any reason to be concerned about whom he passed. It now became important. Between the time of the accident and the arrival of help it had not rained enough to wash away the tracks of tyres on the road. The gendarmes must have been interested in that. Likewise Benezech and his men.

Lambert had read in the newspapers about amazing reconstructions of accidents of which there had been no witness. It would be known immediately that the bus, which had been going downhill, had made a desperate manœuvre to avoid another car which was in the middle of the road and which, instead of pulling over, had skidded even further to the left.

It was inevitable that they look for that car.

Right in front of the plant, above which was a signboard with the words 'J. Lambert & Sons,' a canal boat was moored to the unloading dock. On its ropes hung linen which had been soaked by the rain. A little girl was pressing her face against one of the windows of the cabin. Her faded hair and flattened nose and the mist of her breath on the glass gave her a ghostly look.

The lamp was already lit inside, where it grew dark early. The man must have gone for a drink at the little café by the canal lock, three hundred yards downstream, while his wife was preparing the evening meal.

The office was closed and the employees had left. So had Marcel, who perhaps had rushed to the scene of the accident when he heard the siren. Being somewhat frail, he had been assigned to duty as a medical orderly during the war, and afterwards he had joined the Red Cross. He took his role seriously. He took all life seriously, and he was proud, in particular, that his elder brother had been admitted to the Military School of Engineering and that his younger brother had been the most brilliant student in the lycée. As for his daughter Monique, where would

16

he have sent her to school if not to the Convent of Our Lady?

Lambert almost left the Renondeau documents in the car. He went back to get them, opened the office door with his key, and placed the folder on Mademoiselle Pampin's table.

Jouvion, the night watchman, was already in his hut, behind piles of beams, bricks, and bondstone, for smoke was rising from the stovepipe which projected above the tin roof.

Someone was walking on the first floor—Lambert's wife or the maid. So that things would be no different from what they were on other days, he took the staircase leading to the apartment.

It had formerly been his parents' home, and he and his two brothers were born there, at a time when the plant was much smaller and less modern. He was at least seventeen when the first bathroom was installed.

If his mother and father could have returned to life, neither of them would have recognized the look of the rooms and the way they were furnished. His mother had been the first to go, ten years before; it was only three years since old Lambert had died. Not of old age or sickness, but as a result of a fall from an unbalanced beam sixty feet from the ground. To the very end, active work had been his pride and joy. He would wave the young men aside and say, in his throaty voice, 'Let me do it, my boy!'

Lambert caught sight of Angèle, the maid, in the lighted kitchen. She must have known what had happened, for she was sniffling and her eyes were red.

'Isn't Madame home?'

'No, sir. She left as soon as she heard the news.'

17

'Alone?'

'Monsieur Marcel took her in his car.'

He suddenly felt overwhelmed, as if everything were being directed against him, as if an enemy clan were already in the process of formation.

'Didn't Monsieur go to have a look?'

'No.'

'It seems that it's awful, one of the most horrible accidents there's been. All those poor darlings who were going back to their parents and who . . .'

He lit a cigarette feverishly, the first since the Big Hill.

'I wonder how many of them they'll be able to save. It was announced on the radio a little while ago that . . .'

He noticed merely that the little kitchen radio was on, though it was turned down.

He could not go to bed, could not say he was ill and shut the door on everyone as he felt like doing. He had to behave as he did on other evenings, had to talk, to listen, to nod his head and sigh, he too.

'I'll be back at the usual time, Angèle.'

That meant at about eight o'clock. He walked to the bathroom as usual, likewise so as not to change his routine, washed his hands, and ran a comb through his hair. As he soaped his hands, it seemed to him that they retained the odour of Edmonde.

He was tempted to drink a glass of brandy, the driest possible, in order to calm his nerves, but he had the courage not to. He liked to drink. It was almost part of his work. After a few glasses, he sometimes talked too much, with a certain pomposity, which he then took for sincerity. Sometimes, at the Café Riche, he would let himself go so far as to bang his fist on the table and roar:

'If only we weren't surrounded by that gang of fools!'

18

Or else he would exclaim indignantly, referring to God knows whom, 'The day everyone decides to stop being fooled by those bastards . . .'

It was agonizing to be walking in the empty flat and then in the unlit office, which he went through as if he were fleeing. He envied the people on the barge who were about to sit down at the table, for they got up at five in the morning. He even envied old Jouvion, who was probably cooking potatoes on the cast-iron cover of his stove.

Tomorrow, the day after tomorrow, he would feel better, for he would know. If they were bound to arrest him, he would rather they did it right away. Tough luck! During the war, hadn't he been in danger of death almost every minute? Or of having a leg shot off? Or of becoming blind?

So?

He would not defend himself. He was in the wrong. Granted! No need to repeat it to him, since he had been the first to know it. As for the rest, that was his affair and no one else's. Everyone makes the best he can of his life, and he considered himself as decent a man as anyone he knew.

He drove off in his car and for a hundred yards forgot to turn on the lights. Though night had not yet fallen, the sun had set quite a while before.

The city looked more sinister in the lamplight, especially since the factories and offices were closed, for everybody was outside, on the pavement, in the cafés, discussing the accident, gesticulating, bewailing, with women crying and children whom they didn't know what to do with and in whose presence they suddenly grew silent.

19

At the Café Riche, however, four men were playing cards, as they did on other evenings, at the table which Lambert had christened the 'butcher's table' because Repellin the butcher was the life and soul of it, the one who took up the most room and spoke loudest.

Opposite them, Lescure and Nédelec were having their apéritif and conversing in low voices, but they had not laid out the green cloth or called for a pack of cards.

'Isn't Weisberg here?' asked Lambert in astonishment. 'I met him a little while ago and he said . . .'

'His wife rang him up.'

'Something wrong at home?'

'One of his friends who had a store in Paris heard the news over the radio, and since his son . . .'

'In the bus?' he asked.

'Yes. Most probably. They don't quite know. Two buses left at about the same time, each with half the campers. The second is still on the road somewhere, but they haven't been able to contact it yet, so there's no knowing which children were killed and which weren't. Town Hall's been flooded with phone calls. Since those people know Weisberg . . .'

'What will you have, Monsieur Lambert? As usual?'

'As usual' meant a pernod, and he nodded.

'I saw Benezech with the Lieutenant of the gendarmes. They both looked pretty sick. The hotels don't know what to do. Everyone's reserving rooms, the papers for their reporters and photographers, and the parents who still don't know . . . When the train arrives from Paris this evening . . .'

Nédelec, the grain merchant, interrupted the insurance agent.

'Two journalists, one of them from the radio, have

20

already arrived by plane. They were almost killed landing in a field.'

Lescure also had children, and even grandchildren, for his two daughters were married. Nédelec, who was a widower, lived with his only daughter, who was deaf and dumb.

They could hear the noise of traffic in the square. It was denser than on other evenings, and four or five policemen were stopping cars from going in the direction of the Big Hill.

Lambert, who had just sipped his apéritif, was himself surprised at being able to ask:

'Do they know how many there were?'

'Forty-eight, plus the driver, a middle-aged woman who they assume was in charge, and a girl who helped her.'

He could see himself in the mirror opposite, among other faces, and also the reflection of the lighted lamps and of the smoke that drifted above their heads. Didn't they have anything else to tell him? Would he have to ask *all* the questions?

He emptied his glass and signalled to the waiter for another.

'Don't they know how it happened?'

'Some engineers have come to help the police and the gendarmes. As far as they know now, a car was zigzagging along the road and suddenly got in front of the bus, which tried to avoid a collision. The bus hit a tree and was literally thrown against the Château Roisin wall. For ten years there's been talk of demolishing that wall, which no longer serves any purpose, and of reshaping the curve. How many accidents have there been on that spot in the last ten years?'

'I don't know.'

'Benezech was talking to me about it the other day. It's a matter that I've studied, too, from the point of view of insurance. Sixty-eight accidents, twelve of them mortal. This time, they're obviously going to do something about it.'

The police station was directly opposite, on the left side of the Town Hall building, the windows of which were all lit up as on the evening of the big annual ball. Behind one of them could be seen the silhouette of Benezech, recognizable by his moustache, and that of a gendarme who had not removed his cap. Cars and motorcycles were constantly stopping at the foot of the stone stairway, where policemen were vainly trying to scatter the onlookers.

A black car on which was painted the name of a newspaper of a neighbouring region stopped at the kerb, and a tall young man in a raincoat rushed into the café.

'Can I telephone?'

Souriac, the proprietor, who was standing near the bar, merely pointed to the booth.

'Have you seen any other newspapermen?'

'Not yet.'

The four belote players at the butcher's table were fingering their cards and chips, though they looked somewhat uncomfortable. But what else could they have done? They had merely muffled their voices.

'I trump! Ten of hearts, that does it, spades, that does it, and, last of all, this nice little seven of clubs which does me no good at all.'

The butcher was proud of what he had done and looked at the others defiantly.

Capel, the history teacher at the lycée, who played

22

bridge almost every evening, entered the café with his measured pace, slowly took off his hat and raincoat, hung them on their usual hook, and, turning to the table, asked with surprise, 'Isn't anyone playing?'

Chapter Two

IT was ten past eight when he parked his car along the kerb. Looking up, he saw a light in the dining-room. Without going through the office, he went up the main staircase. He heard the radio in the kitchen and found the dining-room empty, with only one place set. He opened the bedroom door, mechanically, because the slightest change in his usual routine seemed to him dangerous that evening, and, looking into the darkness, asked, 'Are you there?'

It was ridiculous. The bedroom was empty too. In the hallway, on his way to the kitchen, he almost bumped into Angèle.

'Hasn't Madame come back?'

'She phoned and asked that you ring her at the home of Madame Jeanne.'

'A long time ago?'

'About half-past seven. Shall I serve dinner?'

He was about to answer no, that he wasn't hungry or that he would have dinner out, but from now on he had to be wary even of people as insignificant as the maid.

'I'll telephone Madame first.'

When Nicole was out, he could always be sure that she had gone to see one of her three sisters, most often Jeanne. In their mother's lifetime, the four Fabre girls, who were all married, met in her house almost daily, as if it were their real home.

24

'Hello! . . . Who's speaking? . . . Is that you, Jeanne?
. . . Raymonde?'

Raymonde's presence at the other end of the wire meant
that the eldest daughter, whose husband, Barlet, was in
the insurance business, like Lescure, was also dining at her
sister's.

'I'll call Nicole, Joseph . . . It's frightful, isn't it? . . . It's
made us all sick . . . Poor Jeanne . . .'

The telephone had to be taken from her hands. Nicole's
voice replaced her sister's.

'Joseph? I phoned Angèle to tell her to give you dinner.
I'm staying at Jeanne's. She had the most terrible shock a
little while ago and she's not over it yet. She was returning
from Bonnières with the children . . .'

Bonnières was a few miles from the Renondeau farm,
and Lambert suddenly remembered that his sister-in-law,
who had a small car, went there often to spend the afternoon with a friend.

'Did she come back by way of the Big Hill?'

'She did. Just imagine, she arrived at Château Roisin
only a few minutes after the accident. Actually she was
one of the first on the spot, while the bus was in flames.
It was impossible to go near it. You can imagine what she
went through, with her two children in the car. She returned in such a state that she had to be put to bed. . . .'

He found nothing to say. It frightened him to learn that
his sister-in-law had been not more than a mile or two
behind him and could have recognized his car from the
top of the hill.

'I won't be home late, but there's no need to wait for
me. Are you planning to go out?'

'I don't think so.'

'See you later. Victor will drive me back.'

25

Jeanne and her husband, who had a job at the Town Hall, were the least affluent members of the family, the last to buy a car, a second-hand Renault, and this made them even more eager to use it.

Lambert sat down alone in the dining-room, and Angèle immediately appeared with the soup tureen. He filled his plate absent-mindedly, without looking at the maid.

'Has Monsieur heard the latest news? The radio's been making a special announcement every half-hour.'

He didn't realize that he was eating and that the warmth of the soup was doing him good.

'The catastrophe was the fault of a touring car which, according to the police, was being driven by a drunken driver. The car zigzagged along the road, and the bus driver, trying to avoid him . . .'

He looked up at her and wondered what her reaction would be if he declared:

'That was my touring car, and I wasn't drunk.'

No doubt she would be all the more ready to condemn him in that the only feeling she had ever had for him was a kind of contemptuous pity. She despised men in general, regarding them as monsters, and him in particular, but a monster hardly responsible for his acts.

At the age of forty, she was without charm, without femininity. Had men ever looked at her? They must have, since she had had a child, a boy who was now about twelve and who was being brought up on a farm as far out of town as possible, more than twenty-five miles away.

She had never spoken about him, not even to Nicole, who had learned of his existence by pure chance, and Nicole had never mentioned him to Angèle either.

As a result of her experience, all men, especially men

26

like her employer, were a contemptible breed, and perhaps she felt no more kindly towards Nicole, for she also disliked those whom she called the rich.

The world, as she saw it, was filled with millions of sinners and only a few right-minded people, like herself, who inevitably were victims but who would have their revenge in another life.

'He didn't even stop to help those innocent babes, and he didn't even have the decency to give the alarm. Old Monsieur Despujols had to ride all the way to Saint-Marc before he could finally telephone to town. I wonder what ought to be done to people like that.'

She spoke with such passion that he feared for a moment she might have a notion in the back of her mind. Had the radio mentioned a black Citroën?

'I'll bring in your cutlet.'

He ate it as he had eaten his soup, observing the maid, who, when not addressing him, moved her lips silently, the way sanctimonious women often do. Wasn't this an undreamed-of opportunity for women like her to unbosom themselves? Weren't there hundreds of them in town and elsewhere for whom the Château Roisin catastrophe became a kind of outlet?

He was going to stay at home, as he had informed Nicole, and when he had finished eating he went into the living-room, where he was about to put on the radio. In fact, he turned the knob. The light went on, but, not having the heart to listen, he immediately switched it off and plopped down into his usual chair.

He and his wife seldom went out. Except two evenings a week when they played bridge at the home of friends— Nicole, who did not play, took needlework with her—they remained alone together without exchanging half a dozen

27

remarks. She was almost always knitting for the poor, for she was involved in all the local welfare organizations. He would read newspapers and magazines, occasionally a book. At times, no longer able to bear it, he would suddenly stand up and go down to the dock for a quarter of an hour for a breath of air.

There had never been any real trouble between them nor any serious arguments. The vacuum had been created imperceptibly.

When he had married her, she had been, like her three sisters, a rather gay and pretty girl, and he had thought it would be pleasant to spend his life with her.

Her father, Doctor Fabre, was fond of good living, and their home was cheerful, always full of whispering and laughter.

He would have been unable to tell how it had happened. There had been no spark. Nicole had not become a Lambert wife. She had remained a Fabre girl.

He dared not ask the other sons-in-law how they put up with it. Barlet, the insurance man, did not seem unhappy, but he spent three weeks a month out of town. Soubise, who sold fertilizer, thought only of making money, and Nazereau, the husband of Jeanne, who was the youngest, had a job at the Town Hall and seemed delighted, when he came home, to find one or two sisters-in-law there.

When Nicole's husband went out alone and returned late at night, she never reproached him. She was probably kept informed, if only by her sisters, of most of his escapades, but she never alluded to them.

One night, however, a few years earlier, after a rather scandalous affair with a girl, she had simply said to him, when he moved over into her bed, 'No, Joseph, not that. No more of that.'

She had not wept. He was certain that it had not made her suffer, that perhaps it had been a relief to her. They did not have separate bedrooms because of the nature of the flat. They had twin beds, and when they went to sleep they undressed in front of each other in all simplicity. When he was ill, Nicole took care of him.

Should she have married his brother Marcel? As for himself, would Marcel's wife have been happier with him?

What was the point? In spite of everything, the fact that she wasn't there that evening made the house unbearable. He got up, took his hat, and went to the kitchen, where Angèle was cleaning up.

'If Madame gets back before me, tell her I've gone out for some air.'

'Are you going over there? You won't be able to, because hundreds of cars are coming in from everywhere and they've had to block the road.'

He did not take the car. All he really wanted was to breathe the night air and calm his nerves. He was thinking of too many things at once. His brain was racing, like an engine, and it was physically agonizing.

He stood for some time looking at the canal and noticed that a second barge had noiselessly moored itself to the first. Floating side by side on the still water, with no other light than a lantern on deck, they gave a strange impression of peace and comfort.

The women and children were in bed. Yet, in the silence of the night, Lambert could hear the murmur of voices, and when his eyes grew accustomed to the darkness he finally made out two men sitting near the helm. He could see their bright white shirt-sleeves and the red tip of a cigarette.

Without quite making up his mind, he started walking

towards the Rue de la Ferme, where radios were blaring from almost all the houses. At the corner of a blind alley was a small, dimly lit bar in which the only two customers were standing at the rail and chatting with the proprietor.

He would have liked to go in, to order anything, to join in their conversation, or merely to listen, for he suddenly felt a desire for human contact, any human contact. He knew what would happen if he let himself go. He would not be satisfied with one drink. He would have more in order to steady his nerves, and, instead, the liquor would excite him and make him talkative. He might be overcome by an irresistible need to confess.

It had happened in the case of trifles, things that most men don't worry about.

At the end of the almost deserted street, he found himself, after a bend, at the beginning of the narrow Rue du Vieux Marché, one of the oldest streets in town. It was full of little shops that were squeezed together. During the day it teemed with people, and even now it was far from empty. A small grocery and, further on, a dimly lit herb shop were still open. One could feel there was life in the darkness of the alleys. Men and women were leaning against rails and talking from window to window.

As he walked by, he heard, in the characteristic tone of radio announcers, '*The police have good reason to think that they will shortly identify . . .*'

He did not stop to hear the rest of it. His first reaction was:

'So much the better!'

In that way, they would get it over with immediately. He wouldn't defend himself. He had made up his mind not to provide them with any explanation.

30

What could happen to him? Prison? Would he miss very much his evenings alone with Nicole? Even the late afternoon bridge games at the Café Riche disgusted him to some extent, and the proof was that every now and then he felt a need to lash out.

He wondered why he had fled. Panic had got the better of him, particularly of his flesh. His first and sharpest reaction, the one that determined all the rest, had been *not to see*. He would have been incapable of seeing. Precisely because of his feeling of guilt.

And now, to be really honest with himself, wasn't it fear that was making him almost sick? He could feel a wave of hatred rising up in town and no doubt all over France against the man who was still unnamed. If he denounced himself, would it be possible to stem the anger of the mob?

No one, he was sure of it, not even his friends at the Café Riche, would be clear-headed enough to examine his case fairly. Perhaps in a few days, when the feeling had subsided a little. He dared not look squarely at the people he passed in the street, though he listened eagerly for scraps of conversation. What he heard was not reassuring.

Feeling ran high, and the half-hourly radio bulletins keyed it up instead of dispelling it.

When he neared the quiet Rue Drouet, he felt a temptation to go and knock at Louise's door and perhaps tell her everything. Wasn't Louise capable of understanding? For twenty years she had been his father's friend, in fact his mistress. Everyone in town knew it. Had his father been luckier than he? Lambert was not judging his mother. He had never regarded her as anything but a mother and had no fault to find with her. She had worked all her life

31

without complaining, keeping house, raising her children, attending to everything, the last to go to bed and the first to get up, nursing the others without accepting sickness for herself.

At the time of her marriage, she worked at the spinning mill and Joseph Lambert was a mason. Later, the firm and work-yards were founded on the Quai Colbert. The business kept expanding and the work-yards were now transformed; they now bore the name 'J. Lambert & Sons' in tribute to the founder.

Why had old Lambert taken a mistress when he was about fifty, though his wife was still in her prime? His oldest son was the only member of the family who referred to the matter without shame or resentment. Marcel, for example, avoided all mention of Louise and had openly snubbed her at the funeral. The family pretended to think that she had acted only out of self-interest, though they knew quite well that this was untrue. When the father first met her, she was a typist in the office of Aubrun, the notary, and she remained there until the latter's death. She must have been about thirty at the time, twenty years younger than her lover, and in spite of her limp was an attractive woman. Her eyes in particular were beautiful, and her shoulders were so elegant that women would turn and look at her enviously.

'He nevertheless built a house for her,' people said to his discredit.

It was true. After a few years, Lambert did build a little house for her on the Rue Drouet. Out of tenderness, or perhaps to amuse himself, he displayed such ingenuity that it resembled a toy.

When the father died, people thought that Louise would be remembered in his will. But she wasn't, and Louise, who was in her fifties, still worked in an attorney's office on the Rue Lepage, where she had been employed since the death of Monsieur Aubrun.

Whenever Lambert met her in the street, he greeted her. He had gone to see her, for the first time, shortly after the funeral in order to be sure that she was not in need, for he felt she had been treated unjustly. When he saw her in her own setting, he thought he understood his father's conduct and spoke of it the following day to Marcel, who interrupted him curtly:

'Please talk about something else.'

Perhaps it was because Marcel took after his mother.

Joseph, on the other hand, had his father's sturdy, muscular build and thick, plebeian features, including a fleshy nose which tended to be shiny.

'What are you doing around here?'

He gave a start, as if caught red-handed, for he had not recognized the voice of Lescure, with whom he had nevertheless drunk an apéritif earlier in the evening.

'I'm not doing anything,' he stammered. 'I went out for a breath of air.'

'I'm on my way home. I've just been in the Town Hall Square. It's full of gapers. I bet they'll spend the whole night there. Benezech is furious about the general hysteria. It interferes with the work of the police. Weisberg's friend . . .'

'Yes . . .'

'Everything's all right! He's wild with joy. He cried on the telephone and could hardly speak. His son was in the second bus, which arrived at Montargis and will be in Paris tomorrow.'

Lescure lived nearby, in an old house with an inner court which dated from the seventeenth century and the

33

portal of which was surmounted with a coat of arms.

'Are you going over there?' he asked.

'I'm not going anywhere.'

'Don't you feel well?'

Lambert felt uneasy at his friend's noticing that he wasn't quite himself, and he was about to turn around and go home. He shook hands with his old schoolmate.

'Good night.'

'Good night, old boy. See you tomorrow.'

'Probably.'

Even the word 'tomorrow' took on a special meaning. How would things stand with him the following day? Had the man with the goats been wandering along the road at about half-past five, and had he recognized him as he drove by? The radio news bulletin implied that the police were on the trail of something. If they were after him, wouldn't they have already come and knocked on his door? And wouldn't Benezech have spoken about it to Lescure, who was a close friend of his?

In all likelihood, the highway engineers knew by now that the car was a Citroën, the tracks of which were different from those of other cars. There must have been at least fifty of them in the region. Had it been possible to find specific tyre tracks despite the fact that it had continued to rain?

That worried him. He had changed his set of tyres four months before, at the beginning of summer. He had bought a standard brand.

There were other possibilities, in fact so many that he had certainly not envisaged all of them. Could he have guessed, for example, that his sister-in-law Jeanne was behind him? It was about three miles from the bottom of the Big Hill to the crossroad nearest the Renondeau farm, and at the crossroad was a garage with four or five petrol pumps.

Had a garage attendant seen him go by in the direction of Château Roisin a few minutes before the bus? He had been driving slowly, and it was for that very reason that he was not in control of the car when the emergency arose. Edmonde had not been talking at the time. Neither had he. He was now almost sure that when he had been about halfway down the hill a horn had blown some distance behind to warn him. The fact that he remembered it meant that it had registered, and yet he had paid no attention to it at the time. He had not kept to the right. His reflexes had not functioned, and that was how the accident had started. He had heard the horn as one hears a familiar sound which one no longer notices, just as he had passed the man with the goats dozens of times without seeing him.

He had not been drunk. Renondeau had insisted that he come and have a glass of white wine in his wine shed, but Lambert had refused a second glass. The fact is that he was capable of drinking two bottles, and even three, without feeling it and without its affecting his driving.

There was, of course, something else, but that was impossible to explain. People would recall certain escapades of his, particularly the one that had made Nicole refuse to allow him to get into bed with her. It had happened one night when he had really been drinking and had taken a girl to the Hôtel de l'Europe. He had known that she was just a tart, that she was one of the four or five street-walkers who operated at night in the neighbourhood of the Town Hall.

She had gone too far, that was all. Either she had misjudged him or else someone had told her that when he was

35

drunk he threw his money away. Humiliated at being taken for a sucker, he had lost his temper and thrown her into the corridor naked, after kicking her in the behind.

Benezech had fixed things up for him. But nevertheless it had been the talk of the town, and for weeks Marcel had looked at his brother with a bantering expression. What *didn't* people say about him? They had quite a choice. He made no secret of what he did. Often he showed off, on purpose, in order to shock people, 'the horses' arses,' as he would then call them.

Wouldn't people start saying that the fact that he had no children partly explained why he had driven away so heartlessly? Perhaps it was because Nicole and he had no children that they had never been a real couple. That was a subject it was better not to bring up when he was in a certain mood.

It was assumed, or people pretended to assume, that Nicole was barren. But her three sisters were mothers. Did that mean anything? Deep down, the question bothered him, and he often swore to himself that he would find out once and for all, that he would undergo certain medical tests.

At the last moment he would back out, because he was afraid. He would not admit it for anything. He had often wondered whether other people—his wife, for example— had had the same thought, and that was enough to make him sick or furious.

His brother Marcel had surely thought about it. Lambert remembered a day in the garden when he had stripped to the waist and was lifting heavy planks just for the fun of it. Marcel had looked at his hairy chest and, with an expression of false admiration, had whistled and said, 'Quite a male!'

The fact is that it was in order to amuse Marcel's son that he had shown off that Sunday afternoon, since he had no children of his own to whom he could display his strength.

'*Quite a male!*'

The Town Hall clock, which looked like a brownish moon at the top of the dark tower, was ringing out half-past nine when he reached the square, which was as lively as on the evening of election day. The Café Riche was mobbed. There was not even a free seat on the terrace, the awning of which had been raised when the rain had stopped.

The air, which was still humid, was warmer than the night before. All the windows of Town Hall were still lit up. The crowd, which was moving slowly in couples or small groups, tended to congregate in front of the newspaper office, on the street window of which were already pasted a number of photographs of the bus after the accident. There were also some shots of the Deputy Prefect, the Prefect, a group of investigators in the middle of the road, and the Police Chief, Benezech, in the company of the Lieutenant of the gendarmes.

On a bulletin board was a typewritten page containing the latest news:

'*Dr. Poitrin and Dr. Julémont are still at the bedside of little Lucienne Gorre, whom they are trying to save. She has been given two blood transfusions. So many persons have gone to the hospital to offer blood that there has been a radio announcement requesting that they kindly refrain.*'

Another page, which was edged with a black ribbon so as to look like a funeral announcement, contained the names of the victims, with their ages and addresses. They all came from the Sixteenth Arrondissement of Paris, for the camp was connected with a school in that district.

By telephoto, announced a bulletin.

And below it were pasted other photos, greyish and all the more dismal, of parents massed in the schoolyard waiting for news. It had also rained in Paris, and some of them were holding umbrellas.

Lambert stood at the back of the crowd, fascinated by the gruesome exhibition and insensitive to the jostling of the passers-by. The newspaper had had time to enlarge a photograph for which it had also found a title:

Diagram of the Accident.

It showed simply the road on which the rain, by wetting the dust, had formed an almost plastic layer. One could see the tracks of the Citroën's tyres and trace its path, and also follow the broader and deeper tracks of the bus as it headed for the tree, the damage to which was shown in another photo.

Thus, it was now known that when the driver of the car reached Château Roisin he did not continue on the main road but turned right in the direction of La Galinière. The gendarmes or the police had only to follow the track on the asphalt. How far did it lead them? The road to La Galinière was not covered with the same coating but with a granular substance. Had the rain washed away the marks of the tyres before it had occurred to anyone to take prints?

There was no mention of this. But that meant nothing; in fact, perhaps something was being concealed.

Suddenly he opened his eyes wide at a sight which in itself was not extraordinary but which for him, at that moment, was nevertheless unexpected. As he stood on the edge of the pavement, facing the street windows of

38

the newspaper, people kept passing between him and the backs of the other spectators.

He saw two women go by in that way, slowly, arm in arm, carried along by the stream of people, and glance at the display without stopping. One of them was Edmonde Pampin, pale as usual, but calm and relaxed, who was walking with her mother. They did not notice him. The mother, who was shorter than her daughter, was a heavy-set woman with broad hips. Both of them had gone out without a hat. Probably, as on Sundays, they were taking a walk around the square before going home and to bed.

He did not quite know why the sight of them upset him so. Perhaps it was Edmonde's serenity. She had merely cast a casual glance at the photographs. The mother and daughter were simply two ordinary persons in the crowd who had gone out for a bit of air on a very mild September evening.

He had a desire, for his own satisfaction, to give vent to his feelings by blurting out an obscene word, any word, the most vulgar word that came to his lips. Was it possible that the girl who was walking so casually, with the face of a madonna, was not aware of anything? Or was she really as stupid as all that?

The words of the mason came back to him:

'*An animal!*'

And a wave of hatred welled up within him, choked him. He wheeled about and went off in the opposite direction.

He had just decided to drink, regardless of what might happen later, but he did not go to the Café Riche, which was too crowded and where there were too many of his friends. He kept walking until he got to the Rue Neuve, where he entered the first bar he saw.

There, too, it was more crowded than usual, but most of the customers were watching a boxing match on the television screen which was set up between the two rooms.

'What'll it be, Monsieur Lambert?'

The proprietor knew him. Lambert had often stayed on drinking until closing time, and it was there that he sometimes picked up a girl. The Hôtel de l'Europe, where he had been involved in the famous scandal, was just a few yards away.

'I'll have a marc!'

He ordered it because of its harshness and strong smell. He had a desire for something low, something that represented a kind of protest, a profession of faith. It was at such times that he would blurt out as he looked at the people around him:

'*Gang of bastards!*'

'How goes it, Monsieur Lambert?'

'All right, Victor.'

'Have you seen the excitement that the accident has whipped up in town?'

'I have.'

'And it's not over, take my word for it.'

Victor looked at the clock on the opposite wall.

'The train from Paris will be here in three-quarters of an hour with the families. It seems there are already more than five hundred gapers waiting at the station to see them arrive.'

'God damn it!'

'What?'

He had sworn between his teeth in a flash of anger, and he tossed the brandy down his throat with a furious gesture.

40

'Nothing. I'll have another!'

'I wouldn't want to be in the shoes of the man with the Citroën. I bet that if he were tossed into the crowd on the square there'd be nothing left of him in ten minutes.'

Perhaps Victor, who had been through the mill, was capable of understanding.

'Got to put yourself in the parents' place,' he continued in a low voice. 'As for me, I also put myself in the man's place because I've witnessed quite a number of accidents in my life. What is there to prove that . . .'

'Shut up, Victor!'

Someone had snapped at the proprietor in a categorical tone and with a hard look.

'I'm only pointing out that certain people . . .'

'I said shut up! Do you hear me?'

And Victor remained silent, though looking at Lambert as if to say:

'What's the use?'

The man who had shut him up was one of the town's shady characters, a former boxer who made the rounds of the fairs in the region and was often in trouble with the police. The minute before, he had been following the boxing match on the television screen. The mere mention of the driver of the Citroën had been enough to make him fly off the handle.

Two prostitutes at a table near the door were sitting and staring. Lambert knew them by sight, and they must have known who he was. One of them, who had a gold tooth, smiled at him when their eyes met.

He was tempted. Not that he felt any desire for her, but as a gesture of protest, as with the brandy. In view of how he felt, why not do something really low-down? They would then be able to go for him. His brother Marcel

41

would be content, and Angèle and others like her would have good reason for despising him.

He imagined what the morning papers would say:

'The police searched the city all night long looking for Joseph Lambert, who was responsible for the catastrophe at Château Roisin, and finally arrested him in a hotel room where he was in bed with a streetwalker.'

Wasn't that the kind of place where most criminals were picked up? He had never thought about it, but he began to understand why.

The woman with the gold tooth, who had perhaps noticed his hesitation, opened her bag and powdered her face without taking her eyes off him.

'I'll have another, Victor,' he ordered.

From where she sat, the girl asked with a simper, 'Me too?'

He shrugged. Let them drink as much as they liked, she and her friend, and all the women wandering around the Town Hall as if they were at a fair!

'Should I?' asked Victor.

'Why not?'

His wife was at Jeanne's place, with her other sisters. All the Fabre girls were there with Nazereau, Jeanne's husband, a decent sort of moron, and, by God, all four of them were deeply moved! And all the high-minded folk in town were crying to their hearts' content. The photos weren't enough for them. They were all rushing to the station to watch the parade of the parents.

'Something wrong?'

That was the second time he had been asked the question, and coming from a man like Victor it was dangerous, for he was more subtle than Lescure.

'Why, I'm like everyone else!' he exclaimed.

42

'Off your feed, eh?'

There was a moment of silence.

'Did you have a look?'

'No.'

'Lots of people did. Afterwards, when everyone started going, they had to block the road. Those who saw the sight came back sick.'

'Another!' he grunted.

Victor hesitated. He had, on other occasions, advised Lambert, in a friendly way, to stop. Why didn't he this time?

'You're not going . . . ?' he asked, without finishing his sentence, but with a glance at the two girls.

'Of course not!'

'Better not. Between you and me, I'm not sure they're clean.'

He almost answered:

'Maybe it wouldn't be such a stupid thing to catch a dose!'

But he didn't. He paid immediately, feeling that things were going wrong, that he had to get home as fast as possible.

In the street, he kept repeating to himself in an undertone, 'I've got to get home, I've got to get home . . .'

He was fed up with everything, with his wife, with his brother Marcel, with the girls in the bar and the bridge players, with the town, with the newspapermen and photographers, fed up with the radio, with the gapers who wandered about with an innocent look, with the women who cried and with Victor who gave advice. He was fed up with himself, fed up with being a man.

Chapter Three

JUST as Lambert arrived at the gate of the plant, a figure emerged from the shadow. Lambert was not startled. He reached into his pocket mechanically, took out his package of cigarettes, and handed it to Jouvion.

'Keep it.'

'Thank you, Monsieur Lambert. Good night.'

And the night watchman disappeared into his realm of bricks, beams, and trucks, at the back of which a small lamp was shining in his shack.

It was a tradition, when Lambert got back at night, to give him two or three cigarettes. The old man did not smoke them but made a quid of them and chewed it. With his shapeless hat and floppy jacket, he resembled the tramps on the quays of Paris and, like them, put old newspapers under his shirt in winter to keep warm when he made his rounds.

Perhaps he was a former tramp and had come to the plant in search of security. He shaved once a year, in the spring, the same day he had his hair cut. In all likelihood, he was the only person in town at that hour who knew nothing about the catastrophe.

The apartment was dark, except for a streak of light under the door of the kitchen, where Lambert found Angèle sitting upright in her chair, with her head bent forward and her hands crossed on her lap. With her eyes half-closed, she was listening to a play on the radio.

She declared with a start, as if he were at fault, 'Madame isn't home yet.'

'Who the hell cares!' he answered.

He did not say good night to her. Without another word, he walked away, convinced that he had just given her great pleasure. She needed to feel that she was a victim of men's callousness. That was why she spent her evenings in the kitchen on an uncomfortable chair. Nobody asked her to wait up. Even if she thought it her duty to do so, she could have taken the radio to her room, where she had a very comfortable chair, or could have stretched out in bed.

He undressed, spent a moment in the bathroom, where he looked at himself sternly in the mirror, and then, with the taste of brandy still in his mouth, fell into a deep sleep. Later, the light went on. He half-opened his eyes and saw Nicole undressing, but when she turned her head towards him, he pretended to be sleeping so as not to have to talk to her. In fact, he fell asleep again before she got into bed, and he did not waken until six o'clock.

Like his father, he did not need an alarm clock, and he liked to be the first one up in the house. Noiselessly, without lighting a lamp, he put on a pair of trousers, a shirt, and an old jacket and went to the kitchen to make coffee. He did not have a hangover. He had never had one. There was only the aftertaste of the brandy, which disappeared when he had his coffee and smoked his first cigarette.

In the early days, Angèle had made a point of getting up to prepare his coffee. Had she continued, that would have been an additional reason for thinking she was being exploited. For weeks he had found her in the kitchen before he got there, and he had had to lose his temper so that she would stop spoiling the best moment of his day.

45

The sky was grey, as it had been the day before, though a lighter grey, and people were already busy on the decks of the two barges.

Lambert went downstairs, his bare feet in slippers, without a tie, his hair uncombed, as he had seen his father do for so many years, and, before anyone else arrived, went to the office to consult the day's programme.

Except in winter, they almost always had five or six projects going at once, some of them ten miles away. Certain jobs, such as unloading the barges, were done by two teams so that the boats would not be immobilized needlessly.

Twenty years before, the plant had occupied only the site of the first yard, the one on which the new offices looked out. They had had to purchase some lots, then buy out a blacksmith's shop and later a little café where a few couples spent Sunday afternoons when the weather was good.

It was he, Joseph, who was responsible for the expansion. His mother had wanted him to be a doctor or a lawyer. She saw to it that he went to the lycée, where he remained until he was eighteen without passing his final examinations. After he had failed twice, she resigned herself to his working with his father. Like the latter, he had climbed up on scaffolds, handled a trowel, fastened beams.

After three or four years, he already had ideas of his own.

'If we stick to masonry,' he said to the old man, 'we'll never get any really big jobs.'

Their chief clients were the farmers in the surrounding countryside for whom they began to build metal barns and silos.

46

This was a new branch of activity to be studied. New work crews had to be trained. While they were at it, why not go in for heavy carpentry as well?

It was also he who had suggested that Marcel, who was five years younger, attend a good technical school, and the boy was sent to Saint-Etienne.

The two brothers had never had a professional disagreement. Each had his own work and responsibilities. Marcel was, in a sense, the brains of the business, and Joseph the live wire.

And when, after their father's death, Fernand, the youngest brother, who lived in Paris, asked for his share, they decided to borrow enough money from the bank to pay him a lump sum and thereby have complete control of the business.

They had equal power. As for what Fernand had done with his money, they were left in the dark. They had heard talk about his having opened a picture gallery somewhere near the Boulevard Saint-Germain. It was possible. With Fernand, anything was possible. He did not take after either of his parents. With his long face, light brown hair, and delicate movements, he had always been a kind of foreign element in the family.

Because of a threat of tuberculosis when he was eleven or twelve, he was taken away from school and for two years lived a hothouse existence at home, where he spent his days devouring books.

Then he was sent to a boarding school in Haute-Savoie, and when he returned he was so different from the others that they felt ill at ease in his presence.

At the age of seventeen, he left for Paris without a word to anyone, and eight or nine months went by without news of him. Later, he came home occasionally to see his parents. Every time he returned, he seemed more polished and refined, in fact so refined that Joseph often wondered whether he was a homosexual. He had been a member of an avant-garde theatre group which was occasionally spoken of in the papers, and had worked in an obscure publishing house. And he had once written to their father from Capri asking for money.

How old was he now? Four years younger than Marcel. Hence, nine years younger than Joseph. In other words, thirty-eight. At their mother's funeral, he seemed to be the one who was hardest hit. He left for Paris the same evening, after which they did not see him again until the old man died.

Joseph had observed him very sharply that day, particularly at the cemetery, during the procession of friends and acquaintances. He had been struck by the ethereal quality of his younger brother. It was as if by virtue of a kind of grace Fernand had escaped from reality, from the cares of daily life, as if he were not subject to the law of gravity.

Joseph had spoken of his impression to Marcel the following day.

'Don't you have a feeling that Fernand takes drugs?'

Marcel had looked at him with his cold, mocking eyes, the eyes of a man who knows everything, and had shrugged his shoulders.

What good did it do to think about Fernand, or about Marcel, who was punctual and sure of himself and who at nine sharp would be in his office which was strewn with drawing-boards?

Men started gathering on the dock. Most of them were North Africans, poor devils who were badly dressed and were still half-asleep and cold. The office picked them up

48

in the slums whenever there was a boat to unload. It was not regular work. Often, two weeks went by before a barge moored at the landing.

They stamped their feet in the cool morning air, trying to get warm, and some of them slapped their shoulder-blades with broad puppetlike movements.

Finally, old Angelot, whom everyone called Oscar, slowly arrived on his bicycle.

Lambert met him in the yard.

'How goes it, Monsieur Lambert?'

'All right, Oscar. Are your men there?'

'Not all of them. I'm sure we'll need a few more.'

A local newspaper, edged with black, as on days of national mourning, stuck out of his pocket, but Lambert did not ask to see it.

Old Angelot went to the cloakroom to change his clothes, while Lambert crossed the roadway. He stood in front of the barges. The bargemen had already removed the hatches. The boats were each carrying a load of sleek pink bricks which little by little would pile up on the dock in neat columns as regular as houses.

The bargemen waved at him. There was a smell of coffee in the air near the cabin, and one could hear the voice of the little girl, who was being dressed by her mother and who could be seen through the porthole in her white underwear.

Another copy of the black-rimmed newspaper was lying on the deck. Old Angelot came back and blew his whistle. The men gathered around him to receive instructions while other workmen, the regular employees, were beginning to arrive on bicycles and motorcycles.

A quarter of an hour later, work was under way everywhere. Equipment and tools were being loaded on the trucks and vans that were to take the men to their places of work.

'Will you be dropping by to check the framework, Monsieur Joseph?'

'I'll be there at about ten. Is that all right?'

'That'll be fine. We'll get started on something else meanwhile.'

He counted eleven newspapers sticking out of pockets and noticed that things were getting under way that morning less noisily than usual. The men did not call out to each other as cheerfully as they generally did, and there was very little joking.

It was the hour when Nicole got up and had her bath. Breakfast would be served at eight, and then Lambert would also bathe.

To buy a paper, he would have had to walk about three hundred yards to the Rue de la Ferme, and he didn't want to go there in his slippers and with his hair uncombed.

He was both afraid and eager to know. His feverishness and excitement of the night before had given way to a mood as gloomy as the morning sky or, better, as his reflection in the dirty water of the canal. A bad taste lingered in his mouth, but it wasn't the taste of the brandy he had drunk in Victor's bar the night before, and he was ashamed of the way he had hesitated when he had looked at the girl with the gold tooth.

An expression flashed across his mind, an expression he had heard used only by the strange priest who had taught the boys their catechism: *the bitter aftertaste of a bad conscience*.

Since getting up, he had been walking, behaving, talking, and looking at people like a guilty man.

50

He had a feeling that everyone knew, that Benezech was merely waiting until it was a decent hour to come and arrest him. He prowled about in the carpentry shop, in the warehouses, and, as Oscar was still on the dock giving orders to the North Africans, he slipped into the cloakroom to take the newspaper from his pocket.

He did not open it until he was in his office and had shut the door.

The first page was almost entirely covered with the photos he had seen the night before in the display window in the Town Hall Square. There were, however, two which were new to him. The first, which had been taken by an amateur, showed a little girl of about eight standing in a garden with her head bent to the side and her arms pressed stiffly against her body.

Beneath it was the following caption:

'*Little Lucienne Gorre on holiday last year.*'

Next to it was a photo showing a hospital bed and a man in a white smock bending over a motionless body, the face of which was covered with bandages:

'*Dr. Julémont is doing his utmost to save the child's life.*'

The photo also showed a rubber tube attached to the patient's arm.

A sub-headline in the middle of the page stated:

'*A sixty per cent chance, according to the doctors.*'

It was only on the second page that there was any reference to himself:

'*Wide-scale police operation to find the Citroën.*'

He almost stopped reading. He felt like reaching out for the telephone on his deck, calling up Benezech, and saying:

'Stop looking, my boy, it's me.'

51

From where he sat he could see the Citroën that dozens of policemen and gendarmes were hunting for throughout the region. He could see it through the window, against the kerb where it had spent the night. Had any of the workmen, when they arrived that morning, looked at it and wondered: 'Maybe it's that one?'

Many of them knew that he had been to the Renondeau farm and had probably gone by way of the Big Hill.

In addition, Marcel knew that he had taken Edmonde along and knew why, for he had caught them together at least once, not in the car but in what was called the record office. Marcel, as was to be expected, had not said anything and had never alluded to what he had seen.

Joseph suddenly felt most afraid of his brother, not so much afraid that Marcel would denounce him as that Marcel knew. If that were so, wouldn't the simplest thing be to shoot himself? Lambert had a big army pistol which he had brought back from the war. He had kept it in his desk ever since the time there had been a wave of hold-ups in certain cities on pay-day.

Why not get it over with now, right away, without bothering to go up and have breakfast, to take a bath, without having to talk to his wife and then later to face Edmonde?

The newspaper stated that carpenters had worked all night making coffins for the victims, while an attempt was being made, with the help of the parents who had already arrived, to identify them. By late morning, the main room of the Town Hall would be transformed into a mortuary chapel and the crowd would be allowed to file by.

Would he have the strength to go through with it all?

The father of the little Gorre girl was a widower, though still quite young, with gentle eyes and the face of a weak man hounded by misfortune. He had been photographed in the corridor of the hospital, sitting on a bench like a husband in the waiting-room of a maternity ward.

Suddenly the phone rang. Lambert hesitated to answer. He was sure it was Benezech or the Lieutenant of the gendarmes, or perhaps Marcel, who had just discovered the truth. He let it ring several times and finally picked up the receiver because the sound was unbearable.

'Hello!'

'Is that you, Monsieur Lambert?'

He relaxed so quickly that his whole body slackened. He had recognized the voice of Nicolas, the foreman in charge of the work at the pig farm.

'I was sure you'd still be in the office. I should have counted the bags of cement last night. I'm afraid we're a little short. In order not to lose time, perhaps you could send over twenty more.'

Lambert's voice was completely natural. While carrying on the conversation with Nicolas, he skimmed the page of the paper that lay open before him. Suddenly his eye caught the following passage:

'The police have launched a veritable manhunt with the help of the entire population, which is boiling with indignation....'

Still holding the receiver, he straightened up and squared his shoulders. His body grew hard again.

'I'll send over a truck in a few minutes. I may drop by later in the morning to look things over.... No! It won't rain.... You can go ahead....'

When he hung up, he had forgotten about the pistol. He got up from his chair, leaving the newspaper spread out, like a challenge. Since a manhunt was going on and he was the one being hunted, it became another matter!

53

He gave instructions to the man in charge of the stock-room, then went upstairs.

'I'll have breakfast, Angèle!' he called out from the hall.

He sat down at his place in the dining-room, where his wife joined him a few moments later. She was already dressed for the day, for she was not the kind of woman who goes around in a dressing-gown or house-coat.

'You came home early last night,' she said.

He merely said yes, hardly looking at her.

'I stayed with Jeanne until half-past eleven. She was in such a state that we were thinking of calling the doctor.'

'Poor Jeanne,' he murmured, without apparent irony.

'I've just phoned her husband. She's up and about. It seems that the morning paper is so awful . . .' She broke off.

'Have you read it?' she asked.

'Yes.'

'What does it say?'

'I'll go and get it for you.'

That was easier.

'No, no, don't bother. . . .'

He went down anyway and returned with the black-rimmed paper. He put it down beside her.

'Did you go and have a look yesterday?'

'No.'

She observed him more closely.

'Were you drinking?'

'I had a few glasses of marc.'

Without asking why or where, she gave her attention to the photographs on the first page.

'If only they save the little girl!'

While eating his soft-boiled eggs, he watched his wife,

54

but it would have been hard to tell what was going on in his mind. He had a grim, fixed expression, as when he was in a bar and felt there was going to be a fight or when he was about to start one.

'If Jeanne had got to Château Roisin two minutes earlier she would have seen the driver.'

'Too bad she didn't!'

'I wonder how he had the heart, with all those children screaming in the flames, to . . .'

He managed to remain seated and even to finish his eggs, but if his wife had looked at him at that moment instead of being absorbed in her reading, she would have realized that he was trying not to vomit.

'When Marcel and I got to the scene of the accident, the fire was out, but the wreckage was still smoking. Marcel worked with the firemen until nine at night trying to . . .'

He stood up and, without haste, walked to the door.

'Excuse me. I'm expected in the office at nine.'

He bathed and shaved, as he did every morning. As he was about to put on the suit he had worn the day before, he changed his mind. If anyone had seen a man in a dark blue suit driving a Citroën, it would be better that he wear a suit of another colour for a few days. He picked a grey one, changed his tie, and even his hat.

They had announced a hunt, hadn't they? And he was the game.

'Do you need the car?' asked Nicole, at five to nine, just as he started down the stairs.

'Why?'

'If you're not using it, I'll take it. I have an appointment at the Town Hall to help prepare the mortuary chapel, and I promised to go to the market first to get all the flowers I could find. We've divided the work. Renée Bishop is going to make the rounds of all the flower-growers . . .'

He handed her the key without a word.

'Are you sure that you . . .'

'I'll take the small car.'

He had almost smiled ironically when she made her request, for that was the very best thing that could have happened. He would not have thought of it himself.

She was going to use the Citroën for her committee work, and it wouldn't occur to anyone that there might be a connection with the car that was being looked for.

'Will you be back for lunch?' she added.

'Probably.'

'I may be detained . . .'

He made a gesture meaning that it didn't matter, and went down the small staircase. He found most of the clerks and typists already at work. Through one of the glass walls, he saw Marcel, in shirt-sleeves, working in the draughtsmen's office.

They did not necessarily go to say good morning and sometimes did not greet each other until much later, when they happened to meet or when they had work to discuss.

He stopped to say a word to the stock clerk.

'I sent twenty bags of cement to Nicolas this morning,' he informed him. 'He was afraid he might be short.'

'Very well, Monsieur Lambert.'

For most of the staff, particularly the old ones, he had become, since the death of his father, Monsieur Lambert instead of Monsieur Joseph, whereas his brother had remained Monsieur Marcel. It pleased him all the more in that it had happened by itself.

'Hasn't Mademoiselle Pampin come in yet?'

56

He was surprised not to see her in her place at nine-five, for she was punctual.

'She was here a moment ago. I don't know where she . . .'

The clerk looked about him. Lambert wondered, with a frown, whether she was waiting for him in his office. A moment later, he saw her come out of the cloakroom. She looked so much her usual self that he was taken aback.

'Good morning, Monsieur Lambert.'

'Good morning,' he muttered.

It was not his usual tone, but she showed no surprise. She sat down at her typing table, opened the drawer, and took out her pencils, erasers, and dictation pad.

'Are you going to dictate now?'

If she wanted to be alone with him in order to talk to him, he would know at once.

'Yes.'

He opened the door of his office, sat down in his swivel chair, and leaned back, as he generally did when he dictated.

'Come in. Let me have the folder of letters to be answered.'

She put it down in front of him, moving noiselessly, without touching anything, and rolling her body in a way that was all her own. She sat down in her usual place, put her pad on the arm-rest, and waited. She did not raise her eyes until several minutes went by without his speaking.

He was so astounded by her calmness, by her inhuman indifference, which suddenly reminded him of his brother Fernand, that he almost attacked her. Fernand had the same way of handling objects, as if he were juggling them or as if they had no substance.

'*Dear Sir . . .*'

He broke off.

'It's to Bigois and Company in Lille.'

'Very well.'

'*I regret to inform you that, in spite of our comments of* ... put in the dates of my last two letters.'

'July 18 and August 23.'

She said it quite simply, without vanity, without wanting to astonish him.

'Good. Let's continue ... *our comments of July 18 and August 23, the packing cases continue to be defective, which involves a loss of almost twenty per cent.* ...'

'Monsieur Bicard estimates the loss at twelve per cent.'

Bicard, who was the chief book-keeper of the firm, occupied, by himself, a glass cubby-hole crammed with account books.

'I said twenty per cent.'

'Very well, sir.'

'Please don't interrupt.'

'Very well, sir.'

He pulled his handkerchief from his pocket and wiped his face furiously. He was losing control.

'Where are we?'

'... *a loss of almost twenty per cent.* ...'

'Add that, in view of this, we can't continue to do business with them and end with regretfully yours. ... Do you have the Beauchet file?'

'I put it on your blotter.'

'Take down the following: *Dear Beauchet, I am enclosing a copy of the estimate for which you asked and which, I think, you will find satisfactory. I wish to point out, however, that if the total cost is somewhat higher than earlier estimates, this is due to the new customs duty on wood from the north. I thought that* ...'

He called out in a rage, 'Come in!'

Someone had knocked at the door. The door opened. It was Marcel. He put his head in and seemed surprised at finding his brother and Mademoiselle Pampin at work. What had he expected?

'Am I disturbing you?'

'What do you want?'

Marcel looked particularly at Edmonde, somewhat the way Lambert had looked at her when she came out of the cloakroom.

'Has your wife left?'

'I don't know. Why?'

'Because if she hasn't, I'll ask her to go and pick up mine, who doesn't have a car. They're supposed to meet at the Town Hall at ten o'clock and . . .'

'Go upstairs and see. All I know is that Nicole asked me for the car.'

'Are you going out this morning?'

'I am. I promised to drop in at the Renondeau farm.'

Marcel looked as if he were hesitating to leave, as if he had other questions on the tip of his tongue.

'Well? Will you let us work?'

'Excuse me.'

Lambert was perhaps mistaken, but he would have sworn that his brother was disappointed, as if he had been expecting something. Did he really have a suspicion? Had he thought he was going to surprise Lambert and Edmonde whispering like two accomplices?

'Re-read the last sentence.'

'*I thought that . . .*'

He continued and in less than a quarter of an hour dictated about ten letters. When he finished, he was standing up, facing the window through which he could see the file of North Africans, like a long, sinuous caterpillar, going up and down the springy boards that linked the barge to the dock.

'If I'm not back by noon, have the letters signed by Monsieur Bicard.'

Bicard also held power of attorney and for the past two years had received a share of the profits. He was a plump, jovial little man who could spend hours in his chair, bent over his accounts, without feeling the need to stretch his muscles. He was bald and had the pink face of a baby. The only trouble with him was that he had bad breath, and, knowing it, he always had a can of catechu within reach.

'That's all for the moment.'

He was curious to see whether she would finally say something, but she stood up without looking as if she had any intention of speaking, and walked to the door.

Whereupon it was he who felt a need to talk.

'I happened to see you last night with your mother in the Town Hall Square.'

She turned around with a look of surprise.

'Really? I didn't see you.'

'Opposite the newspaper office.'

'As a matter of fact, we went out for an hour to get some air. My mother stays at home almost all day long.'

Someone had told Lambert that the mother made men's trousers.

Edmonde waited, looking as if she wondered whether he had anything else to say.

'That's all!' he exclaimed with repressed anger.

It was too much for him. It humiliated him. He was always irritated when he didn't understand things, and now, after a year of the most intimate relations possible between a man and woman, he still had no notion of what went on in the girl's head.

For a moment, as he watched her leave, he wondered whether she wasn't planning to blackmail him.

He had asked himself the same sort of question in the beginning. He tried to avoid having sexual relations with the girls who worked in the office, knowing that it almost always led to complications.

The day after his first experience with Edmonde, he had watched her carefully, expecting that she would take certain liberties, that she would become slack in her work.

The very opposite had happened, which had almost worried him. She had remained unchanged, so much so that he had wondered whether he hadn't been dreaming the day before. It was impossible to detect anything in her expression or behaviour or tone of voice that recalled the female he had made groan with pleasure.

For several days he had hesitated to touch her lest she push him away.

That was a little more than a year ago, and she never called him anything but Monsieur Lambert. She never asked for the slightest favour.

No sooner was the orgasm over than she pulled down her skirt with a mechanical movement and in an instant was again the calm, efficient, quiet-looking secretary who had just stepped out of her office. Her nostrils remained dilated, like those of a person who feels sick, while her heart kept pounding behind her dress.

His eyes looked for the hat he had taken with him when he left the flat. He put it on and walked slowly across the office. Edmonde, who had gone back to her place, did not look at him.

It was his turn to drop in on his brother, who was bent over plans for a garage.

'Did you see Nicole?'

'I did. She's going to pick up my wife.'

It was the same with Marcel. One could never guess what he was thinking, and today in particular it drove Lambert mad, as if people were amusing themselves by playing cat-and-mouse with him.

Nevertheless, in the case of Marcel he at least knew what his smile expressed: a condescending irony. He was so intelligent, so sure of himself, so superior to that poor idiot Joseph who charged about like a bull!

Poor Joseph! He had made blunders. He would make others, since that was his nature. Luckily, he had at his side a brother who was level-headed, free from passion, and who set things right.

Damn it all, why hadn't Marcel married Nicole, since they went so well together! They could have spent their life in front of a mirror admiring the superior couple they formed. And the two of them might have had children!

'See you later.'

'See you later.'

When he got to the door, he turned around briskly to see whether his brother wasn't looking at him ironically, but Marcel was bent over his drawing-board, and his cigarette was burning in the glass ashtray in front of him.

The only one who smiled as if he understood was a seventeen-year-old draughtsman with long hair.

The idiot!

Chapter Four

SOME reporter or other wrote that evening—again—that the sky had gone into mourning. The Lamberts used to call it 'All Saints' Day weather'. Yet the All Saints' Days of Joseph Lambert's childhood memories were marked by low clouds driven by blustering winds that tore the dead leaves from the trees, whirled them about, and finally dropped them, like toy boats, on the foamy water of the canal.

But today there was no wind. It was not raining. The whole sky was light grey, like a dome of frosted glass that deadens sound, and the people in the street seemed gloomier and more furtive than on other days, as if each were partly responsible for the tragedy of the day before.

Lambert, who had taken the small car, made a point of driving through the centre of town. In the Town Hall Square, he saw the black hangings with silver teardrops that had been draped around the portal. He had a choice of at least three ways of getting to the Renondeau farm but deliberately took the one he would have taken normally, that is, via the hamlet of Saint-Marc and the Big Hill.

Saint-Marc was only two miles out of town. After the kitchen gardens, which were separated from each other by barbed wire, one could see, standing alone, Despujols's little grocery-café with its tile-covered wall that faced west.

He drove slowly, making a deliberate effort to control

his nerves. Madame Despujols, a round little woman dressed in black whose belly stuck out in the manner of country women, was standing near her petrol-pump filling up the tank of a car. He waved to her and saw her, in his mirror, trying to make out who it was, but he was unable to tell whether she had recognized him.

What was hardest of all was to take the turn at Château Roisin, where a barrier had been put up around the charred and twisted remains of the bus and where two gendarmes were on duty, while three or four civilians, who looked like experts, were rummaging in the debris.

According to the morning paper, the engineers had several different theories. Some of them assumed that the doors had been twisted by the shock and that it had been impossible to open them, others that the driver, whose name was Bertrand, had been killed instantly and that no one had been able to operate them. As for why the bus had immediately burst into flames, making help impossible, that was controversial, and the controversy was all the keener in that it involved important interests.

Although there had not yet been any talk of money, it had been announced that the company which insured the bus had sent its best agents to determine not only the exact cause of the accident, but also why it had turned into a catastrophe.

The damages were said to come to tens of millions of francs and maybe more. If the owner of the Citroën was found and if his responsibility was established, it was *his* insurance company that would have to pay.

One of the gendarmes with whom Lambert had often been in touch recognized him as he drove by and waved to him. Interested spectators, most of whom had come by bicycle and of whom there were fewer than the radio announcements led one to believe, stood around patiently outside the barrier.

He started to drive up the hill. His face was red, the blood had rushed to his head. He had not gone more than half a mile when he caught sight of the goats on the side of the road. Their owner was there too, a tall, lean man with exceptionally long arms and big hands that looked like those of some village idiot.

He stood holding a stick and watched the car as it drew near. Lambert had the impression that he paid no more attention to it than to any other car but that he had recognized it. He did not stop. Perhaps it was only his imagination. Was there really a sarcastic smile on the usually blank face of the man with the goats? Had the gendarmes already questioned him as they were questioning everyone who lived along the road within a radius of several miles?

Lambert almost turned round in order to go back and talk to him so as to be dead sure. He had had a suspicion the day before that the danger would come from that man.

He had never heard his voice, he did not know whether the man was feeble-minded or not. People claimed that he ate crows and other repulsive creatures, like another old man who, when Lambert was a child, devoured everything the youngsters brought him for the fun of watching him, including field mice and slugs.

The hill seemed long, and he passed several motorcycle policemen, who gave the landscape a special tone.

There were two others, one of whom was standing in front of the garage at the first crossroads, near the petrol-pumps. He was holding a little notebook. The red-headed garage owner, whom Lambert knew and who had often filled his tank, was scratching his head as he was answering questions.

65

That was another test. He had to act naturally. As he turned right in the direction of the Renondeau farm, he waved and called out, 'Hello!' The young man waved back. The gendarmes did not even turn around. Lambert looked in his mirror to make sure the red-head wasn't following him with his eyes, that the sight of him didn't suddenly remind the man of something.

He would have to act that way for several days, with Renondeau too, who was waiting for him in the middle of the work-yard where the rectangle of the future barn was outlined by the framework. The men were waiting for him before pouring the cement around the metal uprights that had already been set up. He got out of the car and shook hands with the farmer, then immediately went over to the foreman and inspected each of the forms. He seemed preoccupied and grumpy, as he usually did on a job. He looked up at the sky and saw a flock of starlings flying through the air.

'All right, boys, you can go ahead!'

Standing next to Renondeau, he watched the first caisson being filled. They were near the machine, which was making a deafening noise. It was useless for them to try to hear one another. After a moment or two, the farmer pointed to the house and the wine shed at the top of the sloping meadow, and Lambert could read an invitation on his lips.

'How about a glass of wine?'

He followed him to the cool shade where the casks were lined up. Renondeau rinsed two thick glasses in a vat of water.

'Here's to you, Monsieur Lambert.'

'To you, Renondeau.'

'Didn't you bring the young lady this morning?'

His question was accompanied by a lewd smile.

'No, not today.'

'A good-looking girl, I'll say!'

'The main thing is that she's a good secretary.'

The farmer took the empty glass from his hand to fill it again from the cask. Lambert accepted a second drink.

'I thought of you last night while listening to the radio. I thought to myself that if you'd only left a quarter of an hour later, you'd have been at Château Roisin the very moment the accident occurred.'

It was not a trap, Lambert was sure of it. He knew peasants well enough to be able to tell when they were up to something. Renondeau's seemingly innocent remark opened up new horizons for him.

The day before, he had gone to the trouble of creating an alibi for himself by letting it be thought that he had not gone by way of the Big Hill but had taken the road to Coudray. But now the farmer, without realizing it, had just provided him with the best alibi possible. If he had driven at a normal speed and had not stopped on the way, he would have reached the Big Hill about a quarter of an hour before the bus went by.

'It must have been a pretty awful sight!' continued Renondeau. 'I wonder whether I'd have had the heart to look. Oh well! . . . How about another?'

'Thanks.'

'Do you still expect to finish the work before November?'

'November 1 at the latest.'

'Then everything's coming along.'

They shook hands. Renondeau walked off slowly in the direction of the barn, while Lambert returned to his car.

He had done the right thing in not repeating too often

67

that he hadn't gone by way of the Big Hill. If it became absolutely necessary, there would always be Renondeau's testimony, if not to clear him at least to confuse the issue.

What he had to avoid above all was to imagine that they were thinking about him, for then he would be in danger of losing his self-possession.

He drove again in the direction of the crossroads, which was a little less than two and a half miles away. Very few people lived on the plateau. The occasional farmhouses were in the middle of the fields, far from the road. A good deal of the land belonged to Renondeau.

About half a mile away, on the right, was a grove, and actually it was there that the tragedy had begun and not, as he had thought the day before, on the Big Hill when the bus driver had blown his horn the first time.

When he asked Edmonde to accompany him, he had, of course, an ulterior motive, but it was still vague. He did not know where or when it would happen; most likely, he thought, on the way back from the Tréfoux dairy farm, somewhere along the canal road, on which there was almost never any traffic and which he was planning to take.

Hadn't Edmonde wanted to wait? Had she acted with an ulterior motive? As they neared the grove, she had said quite simply, 'Would you mind if I got out for a moment?'

She had no modesty with him. He suspected that she had none with anybody. She had pushed open the door, jumped over the ditch, and, with her dress up, had squatted five or six yards from the road. He had hesitated to join her. He probably would have done so if, a little way back, they had not passed a hay waggon that would have caught up with them before long.

'I'm sorry,' she had murmured as she sat down again and closed the door.

He had smiled and put his hand on her thigh.

'Now?' he in turn had murmured.

What it would be impossible to make anyone believe was that they were not in love or that they were not lovers, that their relations were more like a game which had its own rules, symbols, and language.

She had looked at him without saying anything, and he had realized, from her motionless expression, that that was the moment.

They had heard behind them the clopping of the horses' hoofs and the sound of the big, iron-shod wheels of the waggon. He had driven off slowly, using only his left hand, and Edmonde had stiffened at his side.

That was how they had reached the Big Hill and started going down the slope. He was doing not more than twenty miles an hour, and his mind was not on his driving but on the secret quivering that followed a given rhythm.

Though they were not in love and had never acted as if they were, there was nevertheless an intimacy between them, an intimacy of another kind that bordered on complicity.

It was on that plane that their relations had been established the very first day, without their intending it, simply by the nature of things. It had all started a little more than a year before, at which time Edmonde had been working for him only three weeks.

At the time, he regarded her body not as that of a woman but as the insipid body of an enormous baby, and what surprised him was that, in spite of her vacant look, she proved to be such an efficient secretary. He was almost ready to agree with the young mason:

'An animal!'

One August afternoon, at about five o'clock, when a
large part of the office staff was on vacation and the
weather was hot and sultry, he had gone swimming in a
pool he had built for a friend about ten miles out of town.
He had been expecting a telephone call from Chalon-sur-
Saône.

'Shall I wait till you get back?' she had asked as he was
about to leave.

'Yes, it would be a good idea. I'll be back at about six-
thirty.'

He had not returned until ten to seven and, in order to
take a short cut, had entered by what was called the
draughtsmen's door, which led directly from the yard to
their glass-enclosed office.

There was complete silence in the glass-walled plant,
and he thought at first that everyone had gone, until he
came upon his secretary and received a shock.

Had she heard him coming? He was certain that she
hadn't and, now that he knew her, he realized that even if
she had, her behaviour would have been no different.

Pushing away her adjustable typing chair, she had
thrown back her head and, with her dress up to her
stomach, had put her hand between her thighs.

Her eyes were half-closed and her body was so still that
he would have been alarmed had he not noticed that her
fingers were moving almost imperceptibly.

The heat of the day had accumulated in the office, and
no coolness entered through the open windows, only a fine
dust which remained suspended in the air and shone in the
sun.

For the first time, he had seen Edmonde's nostrils dilate,
like those of a dead person. Her upper lip was drawn

70

back, revealing the teeth in a painful grimace that in no way suggested a smile.

Then her body had grown tense, as if she were going through a painful childbirth, and had remained that way for some moments before suddenly sagging. At the same time, Lambert heard a faint moan issue from her throat.

The girl's head had dropped to the side, and when her eyes had opened she had seen him behind the glass wall. She had expressed no surprise, had had no reaction. She had not quite returned from the strange world into which she had just escaped, alone, in silence. Then, he had opened the door and entered the room. He had stood in front of her, looking at her from head to foot, from foot to head, and she had finally murmured, 'Were you there?'

She did not try to excuse herself. She had no shame, she did not pull down her dress, and her hand was still between her thighs. Seeing her fingers move again, he muttered in a hoarse voice, 'You want some more?'

Her upper lip started quivering again, and he had the impression that he could hear her heart pounding in her breast.

'Stand up!' he ordered.

She obeyed, docilely, and went to him without trying to struggle, without seeking his lips.

Ten minutes later she had already resumed her everyday manner and said, in a voice in which there was no trace of what had happened, 'The telephone call came from Chalon.'

It was he who was embarrassed, perhaps for the first time in his life. He did not know where to turn his gaze.

'The three trains were loaded this morning and should

71

arrive on Monday. And you'll receive the shipping state-
ment in tomorrow's mail.'

'Thank you.'

'Do you need me any longer?'

She was not being ironic but had merely used a stock
phrase without thinking.

'No, thank you.'

'Good night, Monsieur Lambert.'

He had to make an effort to answer in the same tone,
'Good night, Mademoiselle Pampin.'

She had also tidied his office and gone to the cloakroom
to powder her face. A few minutes later, he looked
through the window and saw her walking towards the Rue
de la Ferme with her placid, undulating gait.

Later on, Marcel came upon them by surprise in the
record room. Perhaps others did too but said nothing and
merely exchanged winks behind their backs. He had taken
her several times to the Hôtel de l'Europe, where she had
followed him without protesting, but it had been a disappointment each time, as much for her as for him. She
had not complained, had not tried to apologize. Never
was there any mention of what was going on between
them, and neither of them ever made any attempt to discuss it.

Apart from their work, they exchanged, at most, a few
monosyllables which were passwords between them.

She had not changed in any way. Her life, her habits,
her way of dressing, of behaving, were exactly what they
had been before, and he had not made any change in his
way of life either. He had had other adventures in the
course of the year but they had given him no pleasure.

And Marcel thought he understood!

He was now on the same road he had taken the day

72

before. Again he went down the Big Hill and again he thought that he caught a cruel and ironic expression on the face of the man with the goats.

What did Edmonde think about what had happened, about the way he had behaved? What did she think about him? Had it been anyone else, he would have asked. But her—he dared not.

Why?

Was it because what existed between them was on a plane different from that of ordinary life, of life as one conceives it, as one lives it, as one wants it to be?

It was somewhat as if, at a given moment, for no apparent reason, they exchanged a signal and then escaped.

He was not modest in her presence either. They entered a different realm, a realm which resembled that of childhood rather than that of evil.

Despite the years that had gone by, he still remembered very clearly a toothache he had had one summer when he was about nine. In those days, the linden tree still stood in the middle of the workyard. The dentist had given him two white pills, no doubt a sedative. After lunch, the pain came back. It was very acute, and he swallowed both pills.

'You ought to sit in the garden and rest,' his mother advised him.

Under the tree were an iron table and three iron chairs. The child sat down in one of the chairs, with his legs crossed, while above his head the rays of the sun seeped through the foliage, which was buzzing with flies.

With his eyes half-closed, he saw the water of the canal shimmering. Directly opposite him, on the other bank, an old pensioner, now dead, was sitting in a folding chair and fishing. He was wearing a panama hat and was smoking a long curved pipe which rested on his chest.

73

The boy would have been unable to describe what had taken place inside him, and though Lambert had often tried, even as an adult, to provoke the same phenomenon, he had never succeeded.

Was it the heat, the drowsiness one feels after lunch, or was it because of the pills? He continued to feel pain in his left cheek, but it no longer deserved to be called pain, it had been transformed into pleasure, a kind of sensual pleasure, the first such pleasure he had ever experienced.

From a specific, ultra-sensitive point, perhaps the nerve of the bad tooth, waves radiated, as the clanging of bells radiates in the air. They spread to his entire cheek, his eye, his temple, and faded out at the back of his neck.

He could feel the waves coming and little by little learned how to provoke them, to direct them, as if they were music. The foliage above, with its light and shadow, the slight swaying of the branches, and the flight of the flies, took part in the symphony, as did the secret life of the canal, its breathing, the reflections which stretched slowly, the red float at the end of the fisherman's line, and the white patch of the straw hat in the shade.

In the blacksmith's shop, which old Lambert had not yet bought out, the hammer struck the anvil in a lazy rhythm, and chickens were cackling in a nearby yard.

It was all taking place in a wonderful world that reminded him of something. He tried in vain to recall what it was, but his mother's voice suddenly tore him away.

'Joseph! You're right in the sun!'

The sun, continuing its course in the sky, had finally reached his retreat under the linden tree.

'You'd better come in now.'

He stood up, numbed and bewildered, and was angry with his mother for a long time.

74

It was because of that experience, which he had never been able to repeat, that he did not judge his brother Fernand severely. What means of escape had Fernand found? He didn't know, but he was sure that Fernand had one and that he spent a large part of his time far from the earth.

He had never spoken about it to Edmonde. He suspected that she herself did not realize what she was doing. In any case, she did not think it was wrong, otherwise she would have reacted differently when he had come upon her by surprise and many other times later on.

It was he who sometimes had doubts and felt embarrassed, though he had never in his life passed up an opportunity to tumble a girl on a bed or in the grass.

With the others, he could laugh and even talk about what they were doing. With Edmonde, he did not dare; the idea did not occur to him. And yet, there was no communion between them. He did not seek it. Their relationship was rather one of unspoken complicity—until the moment when, the day before, he heard the frightened scream of the horn and saw in his mirror the huge machine that was rolling down the hill . . .

Was he really and truly convinced that he was guilty? He no longer knew. He had looked at Edmonde, who had not batted an eyelash and who, as she walked arm and arm with her mother that evening on the square, seemed as innocent as when she took dictation.

Was it she who was right? He was annoyed with her and envied her. Suddenly he decided to take exactly the same route he had taken the day before. He had enough presence of mind and was crafty enough to realize that when the peasants who might have recognized him were questioned in a day or two, they would get the dates wrong.

75

He drove to the dairy farm by way of the road to Coudray, found Nicolas busy, and spent a quarter of an hour with him, but did not see Bessières.

'He just left for the Town Hall,' Nicolas informed him. 'He told me that the bodies are being taken to the station this afternoon at four. My wife and daughter-in-law are bound to be there. The government offices and the banks have given their employees the afternoon off.'

'Do you want to go there too?'

'Not me, Monsieur Lambert. I've got trouble enough of my own!'

The Town Hall Square was even more animated at noon than it had been the night before, and there was a long line of people on the pavement in front of the entrance to the mortuary chapel, but there were very few customers in the Café Riche and the other cafés of the neighbourhood, as if people were ashamed to be seen drinking that day.

'Get your morning *Eclair!* . . . Special edition! . . .'

There was still a crowd in front of the newspaper office. Lambert stopped his car to buy one of the freshly printed sheets.

When he got home, the office was closed. Workers from the yard were sitting in the shade eating lunch. The North Africans were doing the same beneath the trees along the canal, and some of them were stretched out in the dust sleeping.

'Will you have lunch immediately?' asked Angèle. 'Madame phoned to say that she wouldn't be home before five or six o'clock.'

This meant that Nicole was accompanying the funeral procession to the station. Perhaps, after all, that too was a way of escaping. He had never really been hostile to her.

She irritated him at times, even exasperated him, mainly because of the opinion she had of herself and because she failed to make allowances for others.

Was she as sure of herself as she tried to seem? Was Marcel really sure of himself?

He sometimes wondered. It might be a mask or, who knows, it might be modesty. Wasn't it true that when he entered a room with those broad shoulders, fleshy face, and thundering voice, with his air of being ready to smash everything, people imagined that he had a kind of aggressive self-confidence?

While eating, he looked through the paper that was spread out before him.

The order of the pages had been changed that morning in order to highlight the latest news.

'*High hopes of saving Lucienne Gorre.*'

Lambert, too, hoped that the child would recover, and he thereby deserved more credit than the others because for him that could very well be the beginning of the end. It depended on where she had been sitting in the bus at the time of the accident. All he remembered was seeing the faces of boys and girls pressed against the windows.

It was unlikely that she had noted or even looked at the number on his licence plate, but perhaps she had seen him and, even more important, perhaps she had seen Edmonde.

Thus far, there had been talk only of a Citroën supposedly driven by a drunken driver. The field of investigation was enormous. But if it ever came to be known that there had been another person in the front seat, a young woman, things would start getting really dangerous. Even Renondeau would not fail to see a connection.

77

'*The police have drawn up a list of all Citroëns registered in the region and, in collaboration with the gendarmes, have begun to question inhabitants within an increasing radius.*'

He wondered anxiously why they specified '*in the region*'. Did they have witnesses or information that was not being mentioned? Couldn't a car from any part of the country, from Paris or elsewhere, have been on the Big Hill at the time of the accident?

He found the explanation lower down.

'*Yesterday afternoon, between three and six, a motorcycle patrol made a routine check of all vehicles on the road at the Boildieu corner, not far from Marpou Bridge, ten miles north of the Big Hill.*

'*The investigators have thus been able to estimate closely the number and make of the cars going in the direction of Château Roisin at the time of the catastrophe.*

'*However, there is no Citroën on the list. This indicates that the reckless driver was not coming from far away and leads the investigators to assume that he lives in the region.*'

He stood up, feeling sick, for that was a direct threat, and he hoped that Renondeau did not read the article.

'Aren't you eating any more?'

He was about to answer that he wasn't hungry, but he didn't want to make matters worse by arousing suspicion in his own home.

'What is there for dessert?'

'Peaches and pears.'

'I'll have them. You can bring in the coffee.'

'I asked Madame for permission to go this afternoon to ...'

He understood.

'Of course.'

'Aren't you going?'

'I'll try to be there.'

'The banks have given their employees the afternoon off.'

'I know!' he replied impatiently.

It had been wrong of him to run away—granted. And now it was too late. No one would forgive him. Should he turn himself in, expose himself to the general fury, become from one minute to the next an object of hatred and contempt?

That would mean ruin, not only for himself but for all those who depended on him. Might as well shut up shop right away and declare the firm bankrupt.

He was sure that if he gave himself up even Marcel would blame him for being a coward, because it would mean ruin for him too.

And what about Nicole? He tried to imagine what Nicole would advise him to do, and he could hear her voice answering, *'Why don't you go to a father confessor and ask for advice—for example, Father Barbe?'*

Father Barbe was her own confessor. He was a Dominican who was also the spiritual director of the other three Fabre sisters and therefore probably knew something about him. The priest was a good-looking man, and his white gown emphasized his distinguished bearing. When he passed Lambert in the street, he never failed to greet him, and Lambert returned his greeting.

He had nothing against Father Barbe or against the religion in which he had been brought up, and he had been a choirboy for a long time. To put himself in the hands of the Dominican was nevertheless too easy a solution, just as it would have seemed to him, at the present time, cowardly to turn himself in.

Wasn't it harder to stick it out, to say nothing, without help, without external comfort, and to try to avoid the traps that were being set?

He was as fond of children as anyone, and he would be haunted all his life by the memory of the contracted features of the bus driver, by the carefree faces of the boys and girls behind the windows.

All his life, he would imagine that he could hear their screams in the blazing furnace, screams from which he had fled, but which the newspapers spoke of so blatantly, as did the high-minded people he met.

Tomorrow, this evening, things would be normal again in town. In a little while, the train would be taking the coffins to Paris. In a few days, the wreckage of the bus that had smashed the Château Roisin wall would be removed.

The police and gendarmes would continue their investigation. Little Lucienne Gorre, if she recovered, would return to Paris with her father.

Little by little, people would forget, but not he. The memory of two or three minutes, not even that, of a few seconds, would cloud his whole existence.

He did not even have the comfort of seeing his anguish reflected in the eyes of Edmonde, on whom the catastrophe seemed to have left no mark.

For the time being, he was not even able to fall back on drinking, lest he betray himself. He had to control his gestures, his voice, the look on his face. And if he expected to get out of it by pretending that he had to leave town on business, that would be the best way of arousing suspicion.

He flung himself on his bed, intending to take a nap, something he had not done since the vacation he had spent with his wife at Saint-Tropez. Contrary to what he expected, he fell asleep almost immediately and did not awaken until he heard the door open. He sat up in bed and was surprised to see his brother standing in front of him. Marcel seemed to be as surprised as he.

'I've been looking for you everywhere.'

'What time is it?'

'A quarter-past three.'

'I saw your car down below, but not finding you anywhere I thought you'd walked to town.'

'I took a nap.'

'I wanted to consult you. I finally decided by myself to give the office staff the afternoon off. Most firms ...'

'I know.'

'It was impossible to let the workmen off at the last minute. . . .'

'Of course.'

He had got out of bed feeling stiff all over and started walking to the bathroom in order to wash his face with cold water.

'I didn't see Angèle in the kitchen. . . .'

'She went too.'

'Aren't you going?'

He did not answer.

'The procession is leaving the Town Hall at four o'clock'.

He wiped his face. Marcel still did not leave.

'Joseph!' he exclaimed after a moment's hesitation.

'Yes?'

He felt that this was the really big moment, and, unexpectedly, he felt strong enough to take care of himself.

The immediate danger restored his calmness and self-control, perhaps because he was facing up to Marcel.

'Well, I'm listening.'

'Look at me.'

'All right.'

He looked him in the face, still holding the bath towel.

'Is it you?'

'No.'

He said it with such conviction and simplicity that he saw a change come over his brother's face. Marcel's features relaxed.

'You realize it's a serious matter, don't you?'

'It would be hard not to.'

'Are you sure you're telling me the truth?'

'Absolutely sure. You can go and join the procession in peace.'

'Aren't you coming?'

'No.'

'Why?'

'Because I've had enough as it is.'

Marcel stared at his brother once again, and, before going off, murmured, as if reluctantly, 'I believe you.'

At the door, he stopped and turned around.

'I hope you won't hold it against me for having thought that.'

'Of course not.'

Lambert had the audacity to add, 'It could very well have happened to me.'

He had never lied so well in his life, and never had it been so hard for him to lie. He heard his brother's footsteps on the stairs, the opening and closing of doors, and then the sound of a car getting under way.

He was alone in the building. The metal saw was buzzing at the back of the shop. Outside, the North Africans were still following each other in Indian file up and down the planks between the barge and the dock.

Edmonde must have left too, like the others. It was a good thing she had.

He remained for a long time with his forehead against the window, vaguely watching the dockers go up and down. Then he put a cigarette between his lips. As he lit it, a kind of overflow rose to his throat from his chest, and he burst into tears, still standing with his arms dangling, and looking out at the canal which was distorted by the tears in his eyes.

He was alone and had no need to hide his face.

Chapter Five

WHEN he entered the Café Riche at seven o'clock, the atmosphere was different. It was as if the crowd had exhausted its stock of emotion. After only twenty-four hours of almost continuous commiseration, above all after the solemnity of the ceremony at the station, people were exhausted and empty-headed and were in a hurry to be home and get back to their petty, everyday worries.

The streets and the Town Hall Square, where the drapes had already been taken down, were almost empty. Five or six persons at most were standing in front of the newspaper office reading the latest bulletin about Lucienne Gorre, whose state continued to be satisfactory. In the café, most of the regular customers were in their usual places, though still somewhat hesitant, but Théo, without being asked, brought them the red cloths and the cards as if to mark the resumption of normal life.

A cloth had been placed on the first table, too, where Lescure, Nédelec the grain merchant, and Capel the history teacher had been waiting for Lambert to come and be a fourth.

'Were you there?' asked Lescure as he took his place on the seat against the wall.

He and Capel, who had gone to school together, were the only ones who used the familiar *tu*.

'No,' said Capel.

'Neither was I. It seems that for once the town council did things right.'

84

Weisberg was not present. He turned up less regularly than the others and at times arrived only towards the end to play a hand when someone had to leave.

'Shall we play?'

They cut for dealer. Capel was the kind of player who kept his mind on the game and was annoyed by any interruption. Being a bachelor, he lived in a boarding-house, and he was always complaining about the food.

'I suppose,' remarked Nédelec, 'that it'll be some days before we can count on Benezech.'

'Especially now that young Chevalier has arrived!' said Lescure, who was shuffling the cards.

The lamps were lit. At the butcher's table opposite them, the belote players were all on hand, plus, as always, a few spectators.

'It's true you don't know who Chevalier is. You have to be in the insurance business to know him because he's hardly ever mentioned in the papers.'

'What does he do?'

'He's a kind of super-cop who graduated from the lycée at fifteen and who has all kinds of degrees. He's an inspector for the company that insures the bus. I caught sight of him a little while ago as he was entering the Hôtel de France. People probably take him for a student, though he must be over thirty. He won't go to see Benezech, but Benezech certainly knows he's here. Chevalier makes a point of never contacting officials. He doesn't see experts either, but carries on his investigation alone, in his own way, whether it's a matter of a jewel robbery, a doubtful suicide, or an accident like yesterday's. It doesn't matter to him whether he spends weeks or months on a job, and it doesn't matter to the company either.'

'One club.'
'Pass.'
'One spade.'
'Pass.'
'Two hearts.'
'Pass.'
'Three no trump.'

Capel got the bid, and Lescure, who was dummy, continued:

'The company rang me up from Paris this morning in a panic. They've got the jitters, and I can understand it. They wanted to know the number of Citroëns I've insured in the region.'

'How many?'

'Twenty-three, including Lambert's and Benezech's, but not counting taxis, which have a special policy.'

Lambert had played his card without batting an eyelash despite Lescure's remark, which had struck him.

'What are they afraid of?' he asked.

'Don't you understand? If, tomorrow, they discover the man who caused the accident and if he's one of our clients, it can cost us hundreds of millions of francs.'

'Hundreds of millions!' exclaimed Nédelec.

'Only about two months ago, the court of Riom awarded damages of fifteen million to the widow of a gatekeeper who'd been killed by a truck as he was closing the level-crossing. Multiply that by forty-eight victims. Add the driver and the two women. That's enough to put the company out of business.'

'Your play, Lambert,' growled Capel. 'There's a lot of gab this evening.'

'Excuse me. What's been played?'

'Hearts.'

They threw down a few cards in silence.

'That's why the others have sent Chevalier,' resumed Lescure, in spite of himself. He was worried.

'In order to establish at the very beginning,' ventured Lambert, 'that the driver of the Citroën is responsible for the accident?'

'To try, in any case.'

'So that if they find him, the two companies will fight it out?'

'Probably.'

'And each of them will try to prove that the other party was responsible?'

It was so obvious to Lescure that he merely shrugged.

'And what if they don't find him?' continued Lambert.

'At any rate, the case will go to the courts and the thing will drag on for at least two years, maybe more.'

'Gentlemen, don't you think that you're much more concerned with insurance than with bridge?'

Capel, who had missed his three no-trump by one trick, was in a bad humour.

'Whose deal?'

'Whoever wants it, as usual.'

Lambert stayed in the game, but he was more concerned with Lescure's comments than with his cards. He had had to make an effort a few minutes before not to burst with indignation and blurt out, as he did periodically, a resounding: 'Gang of bastards!'

For them it was no longer a matter of dead children, of a little girl who might be disabled for the rest of her life, but of how many millions of francs were involved. The question was not to determine responsibility in the name of justice, but to know who would pay.

An inspector, their high and mighty Chevalier, who was

already on the spot, was careful not to get in touch with the officials so as to be free to work on his own.

Lambert had a burning question that he could not bring himself to ask.

'*Well now*,' he felt like saying to Lescure, '*suppose the driver of the Citroën goes to see you and admits that he caused the accident out of negligence . . .*'

He was sure that Lescure was an honest man, but he had been working for the company for thirty years and depended on it.

'What happens in such a case? He's one of your clients, and if he goes to Benezech with his story, it may, as you've just said, cost you hundreds of millions . . .'

In all likelihood, the big shots of the company in Paris were also what were called honest people.

He suddenly smiled—which he had not done for twenty-four hours—with a smile that was both cruel and bitter. He was imagining Lescure's frantic telephone call to his bosses. Or rather, no—he would not phone, because the matter was too important to run the risk of an indiscretion.

He would probably beg the other person to say nothing for a day or two and would take the next train to Paris.

'Next?'

Lambert was in a state of mind in which he would have liked to try the experiment, out of curiosity.

'Spades, Lambert!'

'I'm sorry.'

Would the company likewise ask him to say nothing, and would it go so far as to send one of its own inspectors also an expert, to get in Chevalier's way so as to confuse the issue?

Perhaps not. There was obviously no way of his know-

88

ing. Would they ask him not to mention his passenger and to say nothing about what they were doing when the accident occurred?

'Lescure, why did you put your king on my ace?'

Lescure's thoughts were elsewhere, and Capel was getting nervous. The butcher at the other table, who was on his fourth or fifth apéritif, was talking more and more loudly and rapping the table with his fist.

If Lambert had gone to the Café Riche, it was because he had been unable to stay in the empty house any longer. At one point, he had poured himself a big glass of cognac and, after drinking it, had reached out for the bottle to have another. He had resisted only at the last moment.

Never had he felt such a desire to get drunk.

Nicole would be home late. Angèle, dressed all in black, including black gloves, and with a veil over her face, had returned at a quarter to six with the expression she usually wore on Sundays when she came back from Mass.

'You made a mistake in not going.'

She had added, in a state of ecstasy, 'It was so beautiful, so touching! With the children from the church clubs and the boy scouts who were lined up in front of the station ...'

In a little while, he would go home and have dinner with his wife. Then, since it was not one of their nights out, they would spend the evening in the living-room.

The prospect made him feel like drinking again, and he was furious at being unable to do so without talking too much. He had cautiously had only one apéritif at the Café Riche and was determined to have no more.

Sitting against the wall, he saw himself as a kind of exile, and he began to hate those more or less florid, more or less shapeless faces which were there in front of him every evening, those starched or soft collars, those voices whose loudness changed with the time of day. Capel in particular irritated him, for no reason at all, and he saw the teacher's face as that of a rat.

Customers went in and out. He knew most of them and waved to them or greeted them with a grunt. One of his clients came over and talked to him in a low voice about a roof that needed repairing, and, in order to rile the history teacher, who had nervous tics, Lambert dragged the conversation out as long as possible.

While he was talking, a young woman entered. The bridge players could smell her perfume as she went by. He knew her too. Her name was Léa. He was not the only one in the café who knew her intimately. The difference between him and the others was that they didn't admit it.

She had nothing in common with the girls one met in Victor's bar, like the one with the gold tooth, and even less with those who prowled around the Town Hall at night. Nor was she like the hostesses at the Blue Mill, the night club with the moonlight atmosphere which had opened six months before and where there were never more than two or three shamefaced customers.

There had been others before her, a good dozen, if Lambert counted correctly, who had hung out in the Café Riche with the consent of the proprietor and the tacit permission of Benezech. They would spend a few weeks or months in town and suddenly disappear without anyone's knowing whether it was because they had gone off with some stranger or because they did not make a living.

Léa had been holding out for a year. She was a plump, gay, appetizing girl whose clothes were discreetly suggestive. She gave the impression of being a kept woman rather than a professional.

Lambert had gone off with her two or three times—
90

three, to be exact—the last two times in everyone's presence. He had sat down at her table after the bridge game, and they had left the café together. The others must have gone about it differently. They probably nodded to her on their way to the cloakroom and then joined her outside.

'Gentlemen, I ask you to be so kind as to keep your mind on the game,' insisted poor Capel. 'I said four no-trump.'

He stared at Lescure, his partner, fearing he might not understand and obviously wanting to make a grand slam or a little one.

'Pass,' sighed Lambert.

'Five clubs,' mumbled the insurance agent, who probably did not have much of a hand.

'Pass.'

'Five no-trump.'

Lescure shrugged as if not knowing what to do.

'Six clubs,' he finally sighed in resignation. 'You asked for it.'

Meanwhile, Lambert had made up his mind. He wasn't going to spend the evening watching his wife knit or listening to the radio or reading the papers, which were still full of the catastrophe. He would spend it with Léa, not that he had any desire to go to bed with her, but because he felt a need to be with someone like her, a partner who didn't matter, with whom he could relax.

'Are you playing?'

'Yes.'

He often felt such a need, even with a street-walker.

'I finesse, naturally. Jack of diamonds? In that case, I trump the ace of hearts, I play clubs, clubs again, and that does it!'

91

Capel laid down his hand and pushed back his chair a little so as to puff himself up, for he had not only made a little slam, but a grand slam too, and he now went for Lescure, who hadn't backed him up all the way.

It was Lambert's turn to be dummy. He got up and murmured, 'Do you mind, gentlemen?'

He walked off, not towards the washrooms, but towards the table where Léa, who was drinking a glass of port, was smiling at him and already moving over to make room for him beside her.

'How goes it?' she asked, putting out her hand.

He shook it mechanically, sat down, and glanced at his friends, who were squinting in his direction.

'Are you free this evening?'

'You know very well that I'm always free.'

'Good. Where would you like to have dinner?'

She hesitated a moment.

'How about the Gold Cask?' she suggested.

Though the restaurant of the Hôtel de France was the smartest in town, the Gold Cask, which was a kind of basement in an alley near the market, was the one where the food was best. It was also the most expensive.

'Fine! There aren't too many people there,' he said. 'Here's what I'd like you to do. I've got to be home for dinner. You eat there and I'll join you as soon as I can.'

'You won't stand me up, will you?'

He shrugged.

'Doesn't your wife let you have dinner out?'

Her question almost made him give up the idea of being with her.

'Do what I say and don't worry about the rest.'

Whereupon he got up and went back to his table.

'It's your deal,' said Lescure, handing him the deck of

cards. 'Do you see the customer who just sat down at the table near the cashier?'

He turned around and saw a thin, arrogant-looking man, a kind of super-Marcel, who was giving the waiter his order.

'What about him?'

'That's Chevalier.'

'So what?'

'Nothing. I'm pointing him out because I was talking about him earlier. He hasn't even been to Château Roisin to take a look. It doesn't interest him. But by tomorrow night he'll know the whole town as well as we do.'

'I said no-trump,' declared Capel, emphasizing each syllable and looking at them fiercely.

It went on that way until a quarter-past eight. The teacher was the big winner. The four men shook hands like people who see each other often, and a little later Lambert drove off in his small car.

The inspector's presence in the Café Riche had finally got under his skin, and he had spoken loudly, feeling a need to show off, as if to attract attention. He promised himself to have more self-control and to avoid such childishness. It was essential.

His wife had come home and had left the Citroën outside. When he entered the living-room, Nicole was already there, gathering up the magazines. She was tired and her face was drawn.

'Have I made you wait?'

'Dinner's been ready only a few minutes. Shall we eat now?'

She went to inform Angèle, then returned to the living-room.

'Have you been playing bridge?'
93

'Yes.'

'Are you going out this evening?'

Why did he look for an excuse? He usually did not account for what he said and did, and when he felt like going out he did so without saying where he was going.

'I have an appointment in town with a client.'

She did not ask which one. She knew he was lying, but she didn't show it.

'How's your sister?' he asked.

'She's quite all right now. But her little girl seems to be coming down with the measles. She has no luck, just before the beginning of school. Jussieu is to see her this evening. If she has it, her brother will catch it. . . .'

Nicole said nothing about the mortuary chapel at the Town Hall or the ceremony at the station. There were domains from which he was barred. She seemed to take it for granted that they wouldn't interest him or that he was unworthy of taking an interest. That was the case, for example, with her welfare activity, her committee work, and also, of course, whatever had to do with religious life.

'Marcel told me that you gave the staff the afternoon off.'

What else had Marcel told her? Had he spoken to her about his suspicion and about their conversation in the bathroom?

Why did Lambert care about what people might or might not say? He was in a hurry to get out, to escape from the atmosphere of the house, where, at bottom, he he had not felt at home ever since it had been altered, ever since it had stopped being the home of his parents. Everything was too slick, too bright, too clean, an aggressive cleanness that was not the good old cleanness of his mother. It was Nicole's home, Nicole's order and clean-ness.

Was it true? Perhaps not. Hadn't he himself drawn up the plans of the flat, and hadn't he always dreamed of that kind of home?

Perhaps it was simply that his wife took the thing too seriously, attached too much importance to it.

She herself, whenever she had an opportunity, escaped from it to steep herself in disorder in Jeanne's home, where everyone helped himself as he pleased and where they ate in the kitchen.

'Aren't you having dessert?'

'No.'

'Will you be home late?'

'Probably. I don't know.'

'Don't forget to put the car back in the garage.'

Why did she add that? Did she have an ulterior motive? The day before, he had left the Citroën out all night, and it wasn't the first time.

Although he observed her, he was unable to tell whether she meant more than she had said.

'Good night.'

'Good night, Joseph.'

He always felt something protective about the way she pronounced his name, something that made him bristle. She was, in short, giving him her benediction, or rather her absolution—in advance, for she knew he was going to do something foolish, but she also knew that it was his nature to do so and that he couldn't help it.

That was what her unctuous 'Good night, Joseph' actually meant.

He had a need to be at the wheel of his car and to drive through several streets in the darkness before he could feel that he was himself again, a man, not a child, not a weak or sick creature whom a woman felt it her duty to protect.

He parked his car at the corner of the one-way alley where all one could see were the lights of the Gold Cask through red checked curtains. He opened the door and was immediately enveloped in a warm smell of cooking. Fred, the proprietor, who was wearing a white apron and chef's cap, went to meet him and shake his hand.

'What a nice surprise, Monsieur Lambert!'

Yet Fred knew from Léa that he was going to come. The only other diners in the low room were four blond Swiss, two men and two women who looked like brothers and sisters.

Léa had chosen a corner near the big fireplace, which was enframed with copper pots.

'Already!' she exclaimed, putting out her hand again. 'Did you have time to have dinner?'

She was eating boiled beef with coarse salt, one of Fred's specialities. On the table was a bottle of Beaujolais.

'Will you have a little with me?'

'I'll have some wine. But no beef.'

'Were you at the ceremony this afternoon?'

'No.'

'Neither was I. That kind of thing makes me sick. Last night, after listening to the radio for a minute, I got into bed and read.'

Perhaps he had made a mistake in not meeting her elsewhere. Perhaps he would have done better not to have made an appointment with her at all. Because of the elegant atmosphere, she thought she was obliged to speak differently from the way she usually did. It didn't become

96

her. He looked at her with disappointment, wondering whether he wasn't going to put a bill on the table and leave.

And go where? Besides, she had realized her mistake.

'What's the matter with you this evening?'

'Nothing.'

'Did your friends say anything to you before?'

'About what?'

That made her laugh.

'Because you calmly came up to me right in the Café Riche. Usually the only ones who act that way are strangers in town. The others are too scared.'

'Of what?'

'He asks what! He's terrific! Of their wives, of course! And also of what people will say.'

The waiter had brought him a glass, and he poured himself some Beaujolais.

'Admit that something's bothering you.'

'I don't admit anything.'

'You were different the other times. I could tell you were in a good humour.'

'And today?'

'Am I wrong?' she asked, looking at him with a smile that did not hide her seriousness. She must have felt she was on the wrong track again.

'Yes, I'm mistaken. I apologize. You're not like that, but I'm so used to those who have a desire to talk . . .'

'Only to talk?'

'The rest almost always comes later. But that's not the main thing. What they want most is to talk.'

'Who, for example?'

'Would you like to know? At your table alone, a little earlier, there were two.'

97

'Lescure?'

'Which one is he?'

'The tallest one, in the brown suit, with the rosette of the Legion of Honour.'

'No. That one hasn't ever said a word to me, and I don't think he's ever been tempted to.'

'Nédelec?'

'I don't remember their names, but if it's the little fat one who sells grain . . .'

'Has he been with you often?'

'Twice. The first time, thinking I'd understood, I left the café and walked slowly, stopping in front of all the shop windows. I had to keep going almost to the end of town before he made up his mind. He's pathetic. He's very unhappy.'

'Because he lost his wife?'

'That too. He was fond of her. It's mainly because of his daughter.'

'Did he talk to you about his daughter?'

'That was all he talked about. It ended by being a kind of consultation. I know that her name is Yvonne, that she's twenty-eight years old, that not only is she deaf and dumb, but that she's not like other women.'

Lambert had often seen her in the street, in the company of her maid, but had never heard it said that she was feeble-minded. Wasn't that what Léa was insinuating?

Yvonne Nédelec was deformed, or rather unfinished, without anyone's being able to make out, at first sight, what was lacking.

'One day, when she was only about eight, her father caught her in the act of savagely undressing a boy younger than she, who was crying. Does that interest you?'

'Go on.'

98

'Later, when she reached the age of puberty, she started going after men.'

'Did she undress them too?' he asked ironically.

'Don't be silly! There's nothing to laugh about. She rubbed up against them and went so far that it became dangerous for her to be alone. There was an incident with the bill collector of the gas company, who was caught just when he was beginning to take advantage of her. The maid came in just in time . . .'

Nédelec had never mentioned the matter to him or to the others, and probably nobody in town knew anything about it, apart from Léa, and perhaps some doctors.

They sat there silently while the waiter cleared the table and handed Léa a huge menu on which the specialities were written in red.

'Have you had dessert?'

'No.'

'Would you like to have some crêpes suzette with me?'

'If you want me to.'

When they were alone, she continued in a low voice:

'The poor man had to confide in someone, especially since the doctor recommended an operation to sterilize the girl. He was scared stiff. So I told him that I'd had two ovaries removed and that it didn't keep me from being as strong as an ox or from enjoying myself like everyone else.'

He remembered the scar which he had noticed the first time she had undressed in his presence.

'Did he end by going to bed with you?' he asked, without apparent irony.

'Of course.'

'Was it because you were afraid to have children that you had the operation?'

'It was altogether different. At the hospital, they didn't ask me for my opinion. I was deathly ill.'

'Did you see him again?'

'Three months ago. He was as gay as a lark because the operation had taken place and had been a success. He said to me, "At least that danger's out of the way." Do you want me to tell you what occurred to me then?'

She had started to use the familiar *tu*, which she usually didn't do until she began to undress.

'Go on.'

'You know, it's probably somewhat extreme, but not so dumb as it seems. If the poor old man found a fairly decent boy, not to marry his daughter, because no one would want her, but to satisfy her from time to time so that she doesn't go after whoever comes along ...'

He had understood.

'What do you think about it?'

'I don't think anything about it.'

He pitied Nédelec, to whom, apart from their bridge games, he had never paid much attention. He thought of Edmonde and went on to think of other women and other men he had known, his brother Marcel too, and even Marcel's wife, who, as everyone in town knew, had fallen in love with a young, out-of-town pianist and who had been caught on the platform of the station when she was about to catch the train with him.

They silently watched the pancakes blazing on the red copper stove. Fred was officiating in person. The Swiss turned around in order to follow the operation more closely.

'It's good!' said Léa, enjoying the first burning mouthful.

'Coffee, Monsieur Lambert?'

'Yes, two coffees.'

Then, when Fred had left them, he asked, 'What about the other one, the bridge player with the ratlike face?'

'Well, well! So you think he looks like a rat too! I've seen him only once and have no desire to see him again. He was barking up the wrong tree. To begin with, as soon as he got to my place he said that he was a very bad boy and that I ought to be very severe with him. Imagine, I was stupid enough not to realize immediately, I called out to him while undressing, "You're kidding!" But he wasn't at all. He was embarrassed and very unhappy, and he tried to explain his case. He was afraid of putting it into words, he didn't know how to go about saying it. Then he mumbled that he needed to be punished physically, otherwise . . .'

'I understand!' said Lambert.

He was not disgusted, but he did not laugh either. He was sad. And suddenly he was almost angry with himself for having said that Capel had a ratlike face.

'In the end, he cried on my shoulder and told me about his childhood in some city in the north, I no longer remember which, Roubaix or Tourcoing, I think, and he begged me to be sympathetic. You know, it's not that I'm old or that I sleep around like mad, but I could tell you stories like that till tomorrow morning.'

'Why did you think, when I got to the restaurant, that I felt like talking?'

'Because you suddenly seemed to me to have problems, you too. After all, everyone has problems. I have mine, and if I let myself go I might pity myself for hours.'

'Don't you ever?'

'Who'd listen to me?'

'Don't you sometimes feel like doing it?'

'Let's drop the subject. If you don't mind. Let's talk about you, about the crêpes suzette, about anything you like. What are you planning to do after we have coffee?'

'Nothing.'

'You see!'

He had drunk only two or three glasses of Beaujolais, and yet his chest was hot and the blood had gone to his head.

'Aren't you coming to my place?'

She lived in a smart little flat, very modern and very feminine, of which she seemed as proud as a young bride. She had once shown him about, stark-naked, pointing out the tiniest details.

'Do you do your own cleaning?'

'Who else? I even cook. When you feel like having chicken in wine sauce such as you've never eaten in your life, all you have to do is give me a day's notice.'

There was now a strain between them, and he felt that she was wondering how to put him at his ease. It irritated him. But Nicole was still up, and he didn't want to go home before she was asleep.

'But you're not complicated!' murmured Léa, as if to herself. 'You're a decent sort of fellow who wants everyone to be happy. Isn't that so?'

He did not answer.

'You know who else is nice in this town? He's one of your friends with whom I've often seen you, Benezech, the Chief of Police. You realize, don't you, that I more or less depend on him? All he has to do is lift a finger and I'd have to clear out of town. Lots of others in his position would take advantage, almost everyone. Not him. And yet, take my word for it, he'd really like to. Besides, I may

102

as well admit it, I said to him, "If it's because you're afraid I'd boast about it or that I'd blackmail you . . ." He almost gave in. Finally he said, "All right, my girl, get going!" And he added jokingly, "We'll see about it in a few years, when I retire." Don't you think that's pretty nice? I wouldn't be surprised if he's never deceived his wife, because he's afraid of complications. What do you think?'

He was no longer thinking about Benezech but about himself and Edmonde, for it was true that he too had a problem, that he too had a question to ask, but after what she had just told him, he no longer dared.

'Would you care for an Armagnac brandy, Monsieur Lambert? And a Chartreuse for Mademoiselle?'

He nodded, waited for the drinks to be served, and, while Fred put on his glasses and prepared the bill at the desk, he ended by murmuring, as confused as Capel must have been, 'Tell me . . .'

'Yes?'

'Do you ever play with yourself?'

'Good God! Why do you ask me that?'

'Because. Answer me.'

'I've already answered. I do almost every day, in the morning, in bed, just as I used to when I was a little girl and didn't know what it was. Take it from me—most women do. But lots of them don't admit it.'

She was not triumphant, though he had come round like the others.

'Who is it?'

'Nobody,' he answered.

And he signalled to Fred to bring the bill.

Out of human decency he took her home. He had made up his mind to stay only a few minutes.

103

Two hours later, sitting on the edge of the bed on which she was lying with her hands clasped behind her neck, he had told her all about his relations with Edmonde, except, of course, the matter of the car.

Chapter Six

THE following day, which was Saturday, was one of those days so neutral that we remember them only as a void and wonder later how we filled the time. Lambert must have got up at about six, as usual, gone through his morning routine, made his coffee, dropped in at the office, and then stepped outside to watch the North Africans, who were still unloading the barge, start their day's work.

At breakfast Nicole asked, 'What do you think I should buy for Marcel?'

He looked at her as if he had been so far away that she could not help laughing.

'Have you forgotten that tomorrow is your brother's birthday?'

Not exactly the next day, but the following Tuesday. However, the family had fallen into the habit of celebrating all birthdays on a Sunday.

'How about a book?' he suggested.

That was the easiest and also the best way of giving him pleasure. Whether genuinely or because it was fashionable, Marcel was interested in the history of art and had a collection of art books containing reproductions of paintings and sculptures and even of furniture.

'I'll drop in at Blanche's this morning,' Nicole decided.

Old Monsieur Blanche ran the book-shop on the Rue du Pont. That was where Marcel bought his books, and consequently the old man knew which works he already had.

What had happened after that? Lambert had had his

bath and then gone down to the office, where, because of his intimate talk with Léa the night before, he avoided looking at Edmonde. Then, after shoving some documents into his pocket and signing some papers for Monsieur Bicard, the chief book-keeper, who was to go to the bank for money and pay the workmen, he had driven off in his car.

He had taken not the small car but the Citroën, for he was going rather far, to Verdigny, where they had just finished the new school buildings and where he had an appointment with the architect. It was fifteen miles south of town. He crossed the canal and covered the distance with his mind completely blank.

He had decided the night before, on his way back from Léa's place, to stop plaguing himself, to stop having problems, as she had put it, and simply to let things happen.

Soubelet, the architect, was waiting for him at the school entrance in the company of the Mayor and two teachers. They spent an hour and a half examining the buildings in detail, testing the faucets, the flushes, and so on, and, as he had expected, he had to have lunch with them in a hotel for travelling salesmen where they had reserved the round table.

After that, the Mayor insisted on showing him his house and making him taste his plum brandy.

It was four o'clock when he drove back across the bridge over the canal. Since it was a Saturday, the offices and plant were closed. Without stopping on the Quai Colbert, he drove to the centre of town and went to see a film.

He then spent half an hour at the Café Riche but did not play bridge, for Weisberg was there and they did not need him to be a fourth. He vaguely watched the cards being laid on the table, had only one drink, and returned home at eight o'clock.

It was the night for bridge at the home of Doctor Maindron, whom he had met through Nicole and most of whose guests were doctors. Doctor Julémont, who was present that evening, gave details about the condition of little Lucienne Gorre, whom he was now sure he would save.

Nothing else? That was all he remembered. He had spoken very little, had been rather uncommunicative all evening, and, when he drove home with his wife, had not opened his mouth.

In the autumn, he would sometimes go out shooting on Sunday. But this time he felt all the less like going since he would have had to be home early in order to dress and go to see Marcel. He decided to sleep and did not get up until Nicole had already left to attend High Mass.

He disliked Sundays. The offices and the plant were empty and he didn't know what to do with his time. And he cared even less for family celebrations of the kind he had to attend that afternoon.

The weather had cleared up. When he went to the kitchen to get his coffee, it seemed to him that Angèle's clothes—she had been to early Mass—still smelled of incense.

From his window, he saw a few men fishing along the canal. The bargemen were dressed in their Sunday best, and the little girl was wearing a pink dress and a big bow in her hair.

It was too late to eat. He took his coffee into the bathroom and then shaved. He was displeased with the face he saw in the mirror. It seemed to him ugly, vulgar. He was displeased with his eyes, which were baggier than usual.

In short, he was displeased with everything, he felt uncomfortable in his body.

While bathing, he wondered whether Edmonde went to Mass. She probably did. Probably, too, she dressed differently on Sundays from the way she did on other days. He had never met her on a Sunday. He had no idea of what she did with her time. She lived with her mother, but perhaps she had uncles and aunts, or girl friends.

In any case, it was of no interest, and, if he thought about it, it was in order not to think about other things.

He was standing naked, drying himself in front of the open window, when suddenly he caught sight of the man with the goats. He frowned. His train of thought was broken. The man was also in his Sunday best. He was wearing a dark blue suit, which was too short and narrow and made him look even lankier than he was, a white shirt, a tie, and a cap.

He was sauntering along the unloading dock, occasionally stopping to stare at the barge with the same vacant expression as when he watched the cars go by on the Big Hill.

It was the first time Lambert had ever seen him without his goats. Never before had he seen him in town or on the Quai Colbert, and the man's presence now made him feel sure that his intuition the first day had not been wrong.

The man with the goats had evidently recognized him when he had driven by with Edmonde. Was he hanging around in order to talk to Lambert? The man walked to and fro, slowly. Then he sat down on a pile of planks, facing not the canal but the buildings on which were inscribed in black letters 'J. Lambert & Sons'.

Perhaps it was because he was not holding his stick that he seemed not to know what to do with his long arms,

108

which he kept folding and unfolding. Then he sat for a long time with both hands flat on his knees. He had looked up at the windows of the flat at least once and he must have caught sight of Lambert, who at that moment was combing his hair.

His face, as far as one could tell from a distance, was expressionless. He made no gesture, did not move.

Was he planning to propose a deal? If so, it was better to give him an opportunity to do so right away. Lambert dressed quickly, went downstairs, opened the door, and lit a cigarette as if he were merely stepping out for a breath of air.

They were only about ten yards from each other. Behind the man, the little girl was sitting on the deck of the barge dressing her doll. Her mother was shelling peas near the helm. There were five fisherman, one of them a boy, on the other bank. A slight breeze ruffled the surface of the water.

The man continued to sit there without moving, and Lambert began to get impatient. He walked a few steps along the pavement in order to tempt him. Since the man still could not make up his mind, Lambert crossed the street, and then, the moment he set foot on the dock, the man with the goats hastily stood up and strode off in the direction of the Rue de la Ferme.

Lambert could have sworn that the man had been afraid of being beaten. He quickened his pace and walked about a hundred yards before daring to turn around.

Lambert looked away for a moment and was surprised to see his wife, who had returned from Mass by the short cut, standing at the door. She was astonished to see him there and stood watching him.

'What are you doing here?' she asked.

109

'Nothing. I came out for some air.'

She said nothing more. A quarter of an hour went by before he went back to the flat, after buying cigarettes and drinking a glass of white wine.

Why had the man with the goats come to the Quai Colbert? Why had he got panicky? The simplest explanation was that he had been questioned by the police, that he had spoken about Lambert and the woman who had been with him, and that he had been prowling around that morning in the hope of witnessing his arrest.

But no one came to arrest him. Nothing happened. The sunny streets were almost empty, and the occasional noises that broke the silence sounded different from the way they did on other days.

There was no newspaper to read. He had no desire to listen to the radio. And so he wandered from room to room, smoking cigarettes until it was time for lunch.

At three o'clock, he drove off with Nicole to the house that Marcel had built for himself on the hill, at the other end of town, in a new quarter which was becoming the most fashionable. It was rather a large villa, modern but not excessively so, surrounded by a sloping garden which was wonderfully cared for by old Hubert.

They were not the first to arrive. Marcel's parents-in-law must have had lunch at the villa and perhaps, too, one of Armande's sisters-in-law.

Armande was the daughter of the assistant director of the Banque du Commerce, a local bank that had been founded more than a century before, in which he had started as an office boy. The Motards had other children, three or four, all married, but only one of the daughters still lived in the region and it was she who was there with her husband and children.

110

It was a family tradition that when one arrived no mention was made of the occasion. The visitors were merely dropping in on Marcel and his wife, and, when they entered, they tried to hide their gifts behind their backs and then put them in a corner.

Motard was a rather solemn little man, and his son-in-law, Bénicort, who worked under him at the bank, pretended to hang on his lips, nodding, approving, and laughing heartily whenever the old man made a joke.

Marcel's two sons were there, Lucien, who was a student at the Military School of Engineering, and Armand, the bookish member of the family, and also their sister, who had already taken her girl cousins out to the garden.

Marcel's wife was a handsome woman who reminded Joseph somewhat of Léa, though she was more full-blown, more striking-looking. At the age of forty, she was more desirable than ever, and she knew it. In her bearing and general manner she was less reserved than the girl who plied her trade at the Café Riche. In the presence of a man, any man, she always looked as if she wanted to be sure of the effect she was producing.

'How are you, Joseph?'

'And you, Monsieur Motard?'

Handshakes. Small talk. The women kissed. Everyone was all dressed up. There was a smell of perfume in the air. The coffee cups had not yet been removed from the table on the porch.

Marcel went from one to the other, very much the host. A car stopped at the door. Françoise, one of Nicole's sisters, stepped out of it with her husband and daughters.

It was odd that Nicole's family felt so at home in the house of Marcel, who was only her brother-in-law, and

111

not in her husband's. Raymonde, Françoise, and Jeanne often spent Sunday afternoon there though they practically never set foot in the house on the Quai Colbert, as if they were afraid of Lambert or did not feel at ease there.

Only one of the Fabre girls was on hand that day— two, counting Nicole, of course. The latter apologized for Raymonde, the eldest, who had had to visit her husband's family in Moulins, and for Jeanne, who was taking care of her daughter, the one in bed with measles.

Little by little, the women gathered in one corner and the men in another, while the small children and the older ones remained outside not knowing quite what to do, for they were not the same age and there was no possible contact between the young ones and the older ones.

Before long, Lucien came in and joined the men's group, and his brother went off by himself to another room to play the gramophone.

What exactly did they talk about? Contrary to what might have been expected, very little was said about the Château Roisin catastrophe and much more about jet planes and, for half an hour, international politics.

Lambert sat there grousing, without taking part in the conversation, and wondering whether Marcel liked such gatherings any more than he did. In any case, Marcel kept up the conversation with his father-in-law, and it was he who said at one point, 'By the way, I've made the acquaintance of an amazing fellow named Chevalier who has a very unusual kind of job. He works for an insurance company and carries out investigations the way the police do. Listen to this, Lucien . . . At the age of fifteen,' he continued, turning to his son, 'he graduated from the lycée and then, for his own pleasure, for the fun of it, just to see what would happen, he took the entrance exams of the

112

Naval Academy, the Military Academy, and the Ecole Normale. . . .'

'Which did he finally pick?'

'The Ecole Normale. And, at the same time, he studied chemistry and God knows what else. He's loaded with degrees and he's only about thirty.'

'What's he here for?'

'The bus that was destroyed at Château Roisin was insured by his company, and he's trying to find out who was responsible.'

'Have you met him?'

'At the Bergerets'. I don't know how he knows them. Perhaps through their son, who was also at the Ecole Normale and who's just about his age.'

Guillaume Bergeret was a presiding magistrate. The important people in town and those who lived in the nearby châteaux met at his handsome mansion in the Rue de l'Ecuyer.

'Has he been able to reach any conclusions?' asked Motard.

If Chevalier had expressed any opinion about the accident, they did not learn what it was, for, in keeping with the tradition, Armande came in and announced, 'Gentlemen, tea is served.'

The women had disappeared a while before. When the men entered the dining-room, they found the women and children sitting around the table, in the middle of which was a huge cake with burning candles.

'Happy birthday, Marcel!'

Every year he pretended to be surprised and confused, and kissed everybody, merely grazing the cheeks of the men, as in ceremonies when decorations are awarded. He was given his presents and put them down on an end table

113

because before unwrapping them he had to blow out the candles and cut the first slice of cake.

Was Lambert a monster? There were times, such as then, when he wondered. He looked at them all, one after the other, and found them grotesque. He thought there was something false about that well-ordered scene.

'Joseph, would you uncork the bottles?'

The bottles of champagne and the glasses were on the table. Armande added, with a lilt in her voice, 'You're used to that, aren't you?'

Later, the children who were present and the nephews and nieces who weren't there that day would regard him as the black sheep of the family, the uncle of whom one is a little ashamed but whom one secretly envies. Armand, the schoolboy, who must have seen him go by in the street with women, devoured him with his eyes. His sister always avoided kissing her uncle as if she were afraid of him or of catching some contagious disease, though she kissed all the others.

He filled the glasses, assisted by Motard, who burst out laughing each time a cork popped.

'Happy birthday, Marcel! And may you have many more!'

Was Marcel really happy with a wife whom he had had to catch at the station and who was excited by every male she saw?

Perhaps Motard was happy, people thought he was, and perhaps too that other idiot of a son-in-law who hung on his lips in the hope of someday succeeding him at the bank.

The storm that was gathering within him was probably visible on his face, for he saw the almost imploring look of Nicole, who seemed to be saying:

114

'Above all, don't make a scene!'

He did not, but silently amused himself watching them, listening to what they were saying, and no one noticed— nor did he, for that matter—that he was emptying one glass of champagne after the other.

Armande's gift to her husband was a fawn-coloured leather golf bag, for Marcel had taken up golf three years before, which obliged him to drive a distance of more than thirty-five miles on weekends. The surprising thing was that by dint of will he had become a good player and the year before had won a rather important tournament.

Nicole, following the advice of Monsieur Blanche, the bookseller, had chosen an album of Egyptian sculpture.

'Who wants more cake?'

It was hot in the room, but in order not to upset his wife Lambert kept his jacket on, though he would have taken it off any other Sunday.

Several people were talking at once. The children had all gone off to the garden or elsewhere, for they were no longer around, except Raymonde's youngest boy, an eight-year-old who for some mysterious reason was weeping bitterly.

'What's the matter, Jean-Paul? Tell Mamma what's wrong.'

Lambert had been frightened that morning when he saw the man with the goats. He had been living in a state of fear for three days, and that afternoon, when Chevalier's name had been mentioned, a cold shiver had gone down his back.

What if they came and arrested him today or tomorrow, or any time? What would he lose? This? The cackle that was going on around him? The kind of life he was living?

The bridge games at the Café Riche with Lescure, poor Nédelec, and the rat-faced fogy?

What had kept him from putting a bullet through his head as he had thought of doing? What was there to prevent him?

He hated the evenings with Nicole. In the office, he spent most of his time grousing. Occasionally he would go on a spree, like a soldier or sailor, and would come home all droopy and haggard-looking.

'I maintain,' little Motard was saying sententiously, 'that if modern education is to have any effect, it must reckon with . . .'

With what? Another jackass who had an answer to every question. Didn't he ever feel the need, he too, to unbosom himself to a Léa?

'Be careful, Joseph.'

This time his wife had not confined herself to a look. She had gone over to him discreetly and whispered a warning in his ear.

'Of what?'

'Sh! You know very well.'

His eyes were starting to gleam. There was no need for him to look in the mirror to know it. And his ears were becoming crimson. His nose was shining. It wasn't his fault if he had old Lambert's nose! It was *he* who was now old Lambert!

'You'd make everyone feel awful!'

It had happened once, years before, when Marcel's children were little. The family had been together for the same occasion, not in that house, but a more modest one in which his brother had lived at the time, near the railway. Before leaving, he had had several drinks, he had forgotten why, probably because that day, too, he had

116

felt ill at ease in his body. Monsieur Motard had been holding him by a button of his jacket and delivering an endless speech on political economy.

'You see, my young friend . . .'

He called everyone 'my friend' or 'my young friend'.

What had happened after that? He had never been able to remember, for, while pretending to listen to the old man, he had emptied every glass within reach. Finally, he had cried out, 'Ladies and gentlemen, what a lousy party! I'm getting the hell out of here, and please accept my very best wishes!'

Marcel had held it against him for a long time. So had Nicole. Armande was the only one who had burst out laughing, but her laughter stuck in her throat when her husband looked at her.

Marcel had a hold on her because she had no money of her own. Otherwise he probably would not have been able to bring her back from the station.

Lescure had not been entirely wrong the day before in claiming that Chevalier was a remarkable young man. He had not gone poking about in the debris of the bus at the foot of the Big Hill, but had made it his business, as soon as he arrived in town, to be invited to the home of Georges Bergeret, with the result that he already knew all the gossip.

The men followed Marcel into his book-lined study. Lambert went along, but not before draining the few glasses on the table that were full or half-full. His sister-in-law, who saw what he was doing, smiled at him. She was a real female, and probably he had only to make a gesture . . .

Cigars were handed out. Marcel did not smoke them, but Lambert took one. The smell of the cigars, added to that of the champagne, thickened the atmosphere of family celebration. Albums were opened on the desk. The men bent over them admiringly. Joseph went to the window, and, looking out, saw his brother's daughter lying on her stomach in the sun. She was fourteen and was already very well developed, for she resembled her mother. Perhaps it was better not to say so to Marcel, to whom it gave no pleasure.

Whereupon he thought of Edmonde and wondered, as he had done that morning, where she was at the present moment. At some film with her mother? Or likewise at a family gathering? Or else out with a boy friend?

He knew nothing about her. He had never asked her whether she had a lover. All he knew was that she was not a virgin when he took her the first time.

Was he going to start being jealous?

'What do you think about them, Joseph?'

'About what?'

'The Egyptians.'

His head was already beginning to swim, a feeling that was all too familiar, and his scowl and grim expression were equally revealing. He looked around and spotted on a sideboard a decanter of liqueur surrounded by crystal glasses, an earlier birthday gift. As everyone's back was turned, he poured himself a drink. He tossed it down stealthily, but just then Marcel looked up and saw him.

Marcel said nothing. It was not the moment. Lambert felt ashamed at being caught, and since he loathed being ashamed he left the room abruptly and walked out of the villa. He was fed up. Nicole had asked him not to make a scene, and if he stayed longer he was bound to. He did not meet anyone. The women must have gone upstairs to

Armande's room to powder their faces and would probably spend part of the afternoon there.

He slammed the door of his car and started the engine. The sound was enough to draw Nicole to the window.

The hell with it! Somebody in the family would drive her home. They were now all by themselves and were probably glad to get rid of him. The bad uncle, the brute whose behaviour was unpredictable, had left.

He hadn't the slightest idea where he was going. Suddenly a wild thought occurred to him, and for a moment or two it seemed to him almost reasonable. What was to prevent him from driving to the Big Hill and seeing the man with the goats so as to have it out with him and know once and for all what he was up to?

The man had come prowling around the dock that morning. Lambert would return the visit, except that he would go straight up to him and ask him what was what.

Either he *had* seen something or he *hadn't*.

Either he had spoken to the police or he had kept his mouth shut.

It was clear, it was definite. There was no other alternative. If he hadn't spoken to the police, who had surely questioned him as they had questioned everyone along the main road, he must have had a reason for not talking.

Clear as could be, wasn't it? Lambert wasn't drunk. He'd been drinking, but his mind was clear.

Where was he? Oh yes, if the man with the goats hadn't said anything that meant he had a plan. And if he had a plan, there was no reason to wait.

Clear as day!

He would stand up to him, would look him in the eyes, like a man:

'What exactly do you want?'

He was sure that the idiot would start trembling. People like that were cowards, always ready to take advantage, but as soon as you looked at them in a certain way, they backed out.

Money?

If necessary, he'd give him some, so as to have peace.

How much?

No! It was unwise to give him money. He'd start spending it. Everyone knew that all he had was his goats and his shanty and they'd begin to wonder. The gendarmes would hear about it in no time, or else Chevalier, who already knew the town and before long would know the countryside.

He wouldn't give him anything at all. He'd shut him up some other way. How? He didn't know yet. That was precisely what he had to find out, how to shut him up. It required thought. It was absolutely essential. *Ab-so-lute-ly!*

He was thirsty and suddenly wondered what he was doing near the gasworks, where there were only workers' houses and not a single bar. He turned the car around so brutally that the wheels screeched, and then he tore off towards the centre of town with the thought of stopping at Victor's. He was in no mood to sit down at the Café Riche. He was completely fed up with people who resembled the ladies and gentlemen at his brother's place.

Victor was shrewd. He did not ask him, as he usually did, 'How goes it, Monsieur Lambert?'

He simply shook hands with him, without a word, with just a questioning look.

'Sorry, Victor. Just been with the family celebrating my very dear brother's birthday and it's made me thirsty. Do I look it?'

While talking, he glanced at his reflection in the mirror

120

behind the bottles and felt an even greater dislike for himself than he had that morning while shaving.

'Let me have something very dry so I can get rid of the bad taste of the family. But no marc. Calvados, that's it. A big glass.'

His voice resounded strangely, and he understood why when he realized that the bar was empty. At that hour on a Sunday afternoon, Victor hardly ever had a customer, and he had the television on for his own pleasure.

'Do you know someone named Chevalier?'

'No.'

'A tall fair chap with a poker face who looks even more intelligent than my brother Marcel. If he comes to see you and asks you about me, tell him I said he can go to hell.'

'Who is he?'

He stopped in time. He was playing with fire, perhaps because he was really beginning to be scared.

'Nobody,' he answered in a tone of indifference. 'Forget it.'

Victor did not press the point, and Lambert explained:

'Pay no attention. The damned family's been getting under my skin. Do *you* like family gatherings?'

'I don't know, Monsieur Lambert. I was brought up by the Foundling Society.'

'In Paris?'

'At first, and then, when I was twelve, on a farm in Corrèze.'

'Were you unhappy?'

'I never asked myself.'

'Would you do it again?'

'I don't know. I suppose so.'

'Well, as for me . . .'

121

But it wasn't true. It was better to keep quiet. He was about to say that he himself would refuse to live his life over again. He sometimes thought so and then two days later would go to see the doctor about a vague discomfort in his chest or simply a heavy feeling in his stomach.

At bottom, he was afraid of dying, just as he was afraid of no longer being Joseph Lambert, contractor, Quai Colbert.

'Hilarious!'

'What?'

'Nothing. I'm talking to myself and I know what I mean. Have a drink on me.'

Victor poured himself a bit of mint-flavoured syrup and a lot of water.

'Here's to your health, Monsieur Lambert.'

'Here's to yours. . . . Tell me, just between you and me, have you ever been in prison?'

The barman remained silent for a moment.

'Funny question,' he finally murmured.

'Would you rather not answer?'

'You'd find out anyway by asking Benezech.'

'For long?'

'Once for six months and once for a year. The second time, it was unjust. I paid for others.'

It had been wrong of Lambert to ask. He was drunk, but not enough to realize it. Why, when he got started in that way, was he unable to stop?

'What do I owe you?'

He had better leave. Besides, the Sunday atmosphere of the bar depressed him.

'So long, Victor!'

'Good-bye, Monsieur Lambert.'

He forgot that he had left his car in the square, and

walked down the Rue du Vieux Marché, thinking at one and the same time of Victor, the man with the goats, and his brother. Perhaps it was dangerous, especially on a Sunday, in broad daylight, to go looking for the man on the Big Hill. Perhaps in the evening, when it was dark, when he had gone back to his hut.

Why not more simply go and ring Lescure's bell and announce the bad news to him?

'You remember what you were telling us yesterday at the Café Riche, the hundreds of millions that your company would have to shell out and all that? Well, my boy! That's how it is! The man in the Citroën is me, and somewhere around there's a kind of village idiot who recognized me. Do what you have to. It no longer concerns me. I may go to gaol, but Victor's been there and he's none the worse for it. But for you chaps it's a question of millions. . . .'

He turned round and walked in the opposite direction. The thought of the Citroën had reminded him that he had just left it in the Town Hall Square, opposite the Café Riche. His friends did not play cards there on Sundays. The tables were occupied by families that had been out for a walk and were now waiting until it was time for dinner.

Chevalier was there, alone, at the same table as the evening before, near the cash register, and Lambert felt sure that the man was watching him get into his car.

Had anyone spoken about him to Chevalier? He was not a member of Judge Bergeret's circle, as his brother was. He knew the Judge's guests only by name or sight. A traffic-policeman motioned to him to keep going. He was perfectly willing to obey. But where should he go? Not home, in any case. He was sick and tired of roaming about

123

the empty flat alone, with that mousy Angèle in the kitchen.

'Well, what are you waiting for?'

The car shot forward, then he turned left because it was the easiest thing to do, and since the street led to Léa's apartment, he decided to ring her bell. She didn't work on Sundays either, since it was a family day.

He rang once, twice, listening for a sound in the flat, but he heard nothing. Then he rang without stopping and finally he heard footsteps. A voice called out:

'Who is it?'

'It's me, Lambert.'

'Just a moment.'

It was Léa's voice, but it was as grumpy as his own. She came back in a few moments, turned the key in the lock, and drew the bolt.

'It's you!' she murmured, as if she had not recognized his name a few seconds before.

And she looked at him exactly as Victor had, with a frown. She had understood. She resigned herself.

'Come in.'

'Do you at least have something to drink?'

'I do, don't worry.'

'Were you sleeping?'

'Come in!'

'Does it bother you to see me?'

'Of course not.'

'Admit that it bothers you.'

'It doesn't. Please don't stand there on the landing. I'm not completely awake yet.'

'A problem!' he mumbled, as if the word explained everything.

'Eh?'

124

'I said a problem. Doesn't that remind you of something? The ones who come for a good time and those who come with their problems?'

The flat was tidy, except that the bed was unmade and that a novel had fallen on the rug.

'What have you come for?' she asked. 'I don't go out on Sundays. I take advantage of the morning to do my house-cleaning, and I sleep in the afternoon.'

'Maybe I'll sleep too.'

'Do you mean that seriously?'

He was already starting to undress. Why not? That or something else! He wouldn't be alone there and would have the advantage of not seeing his wife return home with a sad, indulgent look on her face. It wasn't indulgence that he wanted.

'But first you've got to give me something to drink.'

'All I have is vermouth.'

'Bring in the vermouth.'

She went to the dining-room to get the bottle and returned with only one glass. The bottle was three-quarters full.

'Promise me you won't make a rumpus.'

'Have I ever misbehaved in your flat?'

'No, not in my flat.'

'Are you afraid?'

'I'm afraid of the landlord. He wouldn't miss the opportunity to kick me out.'

It was odd: without make-up she looked like a nice wife and mother, even a country mother. He took long swallows of the vermouth, and she stood there watching him. He was sitting on the edge of the bed in his underpants, still wearing his shoes and socks.

'You're a nice girl,' he declared with conviction.

It was not quite what he had meant to say. But he knew what he meant. As he saw it, it was a magnificent compliment, something very delicate. She did not try to stop him when he poured another drink, then a third, and finally finished the bottle. He kept looking at her tenderly and nodding his head without her being able to tell what he was actually seeing.

'A very nice girl . . . Wait! . . . That's it—you're a real sister!'

It relieved him to find the right word, and his eyes filled with tears. He drank the last of the vermouth, while she kneeled on the floor in front of him and removed his shoes and socks.

He remembered neither her undressing him nor his having gone to bed. He did not even remember having gone to the bathroom two hours later to vomit and having bumped into all the walls because he had thought he was in the Quai Colbert and did not know his way around.

Nor did he remember having called her Nicole.

Chapter Seven

HE was not quite asleep, he was not quite awake. He was deliberately maintaining his balance between sleep and waking. It was a familiar trick of his, one which he often used, especially when he had been drinking the night before. And probably it was the liquor, too, that made his flesh more sensitive, that gave his desires a particular form and edge.

He had begun by regaining consciousness at the same time as other mornings and had realized at once, without having to open his eyes, that he was not in his own bed and that the warm, naked thigh beneath his hand was Léa's. He was beginning to remember. Not everything. It was an over-all impression, with a few details here and there. For example, he was able to recall the emotion he had felt the night before as he looked at Léa and thought of her as a 'sister'. He did not smile at this. Nor was he ashamed of it.

He had opened his eyes just enough to get his bearings, to make out a cream-coloured curtain behind which dawn was coming up, and he had dropped back into his torpor, somewhat as he had done under the linden tree in the garden the day he had had his toothache. He felt within him a refusal to return to ordinary life, and he plunged almost fiercely into a universe where all that mattered was the quivering of his senses.

It was, as a matter of fact, what Edmonde was able to do wide awake, in broad daylight, anywhere, when the click occurred, and when he was with her he could do it too. Perhaps she could even produce the click at will.

The universe then drifted away until it was only a kind of unimportant nebula. Objects lost their weight, human beings were merely tiny or grotesque puppets, and everything to which one usually attached value became ridiculous. All that remained in a shrunken, warm, enveloping, and kindly world was the pounding of the blood in their arteries, a symphony which at first was vague and diffuse, then gradually became sharper, and finally concentrated in their sex organs.

They were unashamed that their existence was focused for a moment in that area of their bodies, unashamed of exhausting the possibilities of pleasure.

He was eager to see Edmonde, to make a sign to her, to read the answer in her eyes, and to plunge with her into that universe.

Today it was essential that it last a long time, that he see her with her nostrils dilated and upper lip drawn back above her teeth, as if she were a corpse. He would go at her again without letting her come to her senses, he would invent new caresses that would make her beg for mercy. They would both go very far, farther than ever, to the very edge of the precipice, until they shuddered with fear that they might never come back.

He tingled with desire from head to foot, as if he had been skinned alive. Even the feel of the sheets was voluptuous. Yet he did not dream of satisfying himself with Léa, whom his hand continued to caress. On the contrary, he wanted to be even more excited and strove to imagine in minute detail what would happen later. Not in the office or elsewhere in the plant on the Quai Colbert where they had had earlier experiences.

128

The weather promised to be warm. The bright sun gilded the cream-coloured curtain, and because he remembered the linden tree with the buzzing flies his thoughts drifted to a field in the countryside or a glade near which he would stop the car.

Was it a reaction against his fears of the day before? He was hungry for Edmonde, hungry for her body and the mysterious stages of her pleasure.

He no longer cared about the man with the goats or Benezech or his brother Marcel or young Chevalier. He still had what no one could take from him.

It would not be the first time that he stopped at the edge of a meadow. And each time, when he stood up, it was as if he were drunk with the smell of the damp earth and the odour of Edmonde. Once they had heard a sound behind a hedge, very near them, but she had dug her nails into his flesh and prevented him from moving. Never before had she been in such a frenzy.

He had to be at the Renondeau farm in the morning to check on the setting of the cement. Should he take her with him then or later, in the afternoon, for example?

He lay there half-dreaming. He created the setting, conceived images that made his desire painful, and, as he continued to stroke Léa, she turned over, half-asleep, spread her legs, and murmured in a distant voice, 'Come.'

He said no, and, in order not to succumb, he got up. She watched him with an expression of surprise, but she was not sufficiently awake to feel like questioning him. It was not until he stood up that he realized he had a headache and was empty, but he didn't care, it didn't bother him, he knew that the sickly feeling would soon wear off and that his desire would remain.

He put on his shirt and trousers, then went to the

kitchen, where he lit the small stove, looked for the coffee among the white cans on a shelf, found it, and poured a few measures into the coffee mill that was nailed to the wall.

As he was pouring water into the pot, Léa silently appeared in the doorway, naked. The folds of the sheets had covered her smooth skin with pink lines.

'What are you doing?'

'Making coffee.'

'What time is it?'

He looked at the alarm clock on the mantelpiece.

'Twenty-past six.'

'Are you leaving already?'

He said he was, and, as her head began to clear, she again looked at him as she had done the night before. It was as if she were seeing something inside him that worried her, a kind of sign, as if she were reluctant to let him go.

'Your wife?'

'No.'

'Doesn't she say anything?'

'No.'

'You're lucky.'

There was no point in explaining to her that she was wrong, that, quite the contrary, he had no luck at all.

'Business?'

It was not business either that was making him leave. It was not absolutely necessary that he go to the Renondeau farm that morning.

'The girl you told me about?'

He nodded. What was the good of lying at that point of the game!

'Was that why you didn't want me this morning?'

She felt no resentment, but seemed even more worried.

'All right, let me have a cup of coffee, too. It won't keep me from going back to sleep. Do you remember that you were sick?'

'No.'

'It doesn't matter. I don't hold it against you. The hardest part of all was getting you back into bed. You're pretty heavy!'

'Did you have to carry me?'

'I had to hoist you up and pull you and push you as best I could.'

'I apologize.'

'Don't be silly!'

She sat down in a white chair. It was odd to see her drinking coffee in the kitchen without a stitch on her body.

'Are you going to have a bath before leaving?'

'I'll take one at home.'

'As you like. How about some aspirin?'

'All right.'

She went to the bathroom to get him two tablets. While she was there she brushed her teeth. He drank two cups of coffee and was able to light a cigarette without feeling nauseous.

'I'm going to finish dressing,' he said.

'Do you always get up so early?'

'At six. Sometimes five-thirty.'

She followed him to the bedroom and watched him dress, with the same thoughtful look on her face. Then she accompanied him to the door, pulled the bolt, and kissed him on both cheeks.

'Thanks,' he said as he was about to leave.

He returned her kisses.

'Watch out for yourself,' she said.

131

The remark did not strike him until he was in the street, where he looked around for his car. Since she wasn't aware of anything, why had she said that in such an earnest tone?

There were already a few North Africans on the Quai Colbert. A barge with a red and white triangle painted on the bow was gliding up the canal. The bargemen, who were standing on deck, waved a greeting to the men on the boat that was being unloaded and called out the name of a canal lock where they were probably to meet.

He went straight to the office and, with a certain embarrassment, furtively ran his hand over Edmonde's table as he walked by. He did not want his desire to peter out. The images he had conjured up in Léa's bed were already losing some of their plausibility in the harsher light of day. The scenes he had imagined, the gestures, the words he had planned to say, were becoming less real.

All the same, he would take her to the country, anywhere, and he would enjoy her savagely. He needed to. He needed, above all, to prove to himself that it was they who were right, that they were justified, that there was nothing dirty or guilty in the pleasure they gave each other.

When all was said and done, wasn't that what tormented him even more than fear and all the rest of it? The only moments of real joy he had ever known had been defiled. The moments with Edmonde and those he had experienced when he had had the toothache under the linden tree. It was the same thing, the same flight, the same leap into another world.

What he had once attained with two tablets of a drug, with torpor and the filtered rays of the sun and the sound of the flies, Edmonde and he attained with their two bodies.

132

So of what were they guilty? And if they weren't, why had he so often felt a veiled anxiety ever since he knew her?

Why, when the bus had let out its deathly shriek ...

He refused to think about it, refused to remember it. On no condition would he relive the three days he had just been through. He went up the steps three at a time and opened the kitchen door. Angèle gave a start and looked at him as if he were a ghost.

'Make me a cup of coffee.'

Didn't she regard him as the devil in person?

'Madame isn't up yet and hasn't left me any instructions,' she grumbled as he walked down the hall.

'I don't care.'

That gave him time to have a cold shower and to dress. He was ready when the door of Nicole's bedroom opened. She merely said, 'You're there?'

He did not look for an excuse and gave no explanation. There was now no point in it. Nor did he make any mention of what had happened at Marcel's.

'Do you feel well?'

'Very well.'

'Do you want breakfast?'

'I don't think I'll eat.'

His stomach wasn't settled enough for that. Work was already under way on the dock and in the plant. He could hear the buzzing of the mechanical saw and the regular dropping of planks. His headache had already gone, but there persisted a certain vague feeling in his whole body and a heightened sensitivity.

For more than half an hour he stood around among the trucks and piles of material, talking with the foremen and workmen. Then he went to the dock to be sure that the unloading would be finished by the afternoon of the following day. The planks, which had still been horizontal on Saturday, were now sloping steeply, for as the boat emptied it rose on the water and exposed its greyish sides, which the bargeman was already coating with Norwegian tar.

At nine o'clock, when the employees arrived, he was in his office. He saw Edmonde walking up the quay and, for the first time, received a kind of shock. He grew feverish, and time seemed to drag until he opened the connecting door.

'Mademoiselle Pampin, would you come in for a moment?'

'With my pad?'

'There's no need.'

Did she understand? Did she think it was to be right away? He was not smiling, was not gay, in fact, he was rather grim and vaguely anxious. She closed the door and remained standing. He now wondered whether, after what had happened on the Big Hill, she would again be willing and whether the click would occur.

He paced up and down the office, putting off the moment when he would have to look at her. She stood there motionless, upright, with her hands clasped in front of her.

'I merely wanted to tell you . . .'

He finally looked up at her and had the impression that she was repressing a furtive smile.

'I'll probably ask you to come with me today . . .'

'This morning?'

He was watching her. He was sure she had already recognized his look. What he would have liked to know was whether there would be a click.

134

'This morning or this afternoon. I don't know yet.'

He added in a less natural tone, 'We'll be going rather far.'

'Very well, Monsieur Lambert.'

He had to turn his eyes away because he was looking at her with an almost pleading expression and did not want to be pathetic.

'Do you understand?'

'Yes.'

He again observed her.

'Glad?'

She said nothing, but her eyelids fluttered, and he was almost sure she had turned paler. That was the sign.

'See you later.'

He had just become himself again. He was suddenly happy and felt a need to go to Marcel's office, for he was surprised that his brother had not yet come in to see him. Three draughtsmen were bent over their boards, and Marcel was working in shirt-sleeves.

'I apologize,' mumbled Lambert, 'for leaving yesterday afternoon without saying good-bye.'

'It was a good thing you did, and it would have been better if you hadn't come at all.'

It was the first time he had ever spoken in that curt, contemptuous tone. Lambert felt the blood rush to his head. He clenched his fist and was about to grab Marcel by the shoulders and shake him. But he controlled himself, and his anger subsided almost instantly. He merely muttered, loudly enough for the employees to hear, 'Little twit!'

Nobody was going to teach him a lesson, least of all his brother! He went off to see Monsieur Bicard, who always needed him on Monday mornings for his signature, and

135

then went back to his office with the intention of leaving for the Renondeau farm immediately. As for Edmonde, it was better to wait until the afternoon and go with her to Orville Forest.

At that moment, as he was about to take his hat from the rack, there was a sudden uproar on the dock. Turning his head, he saw one of the North Africans who was struggling in the grip of two others free himself and run like mad in the direction of the alley that Nicole had taken the day before on her way back from Mass and which was referred to in the plant as the short cut.

A body was lying on the ground among the scattered bricks. At first, all Lambert could see was the long legs. He opened the window and yelled out, 'What's going on?'

Oscar motioned to him from the dock to come down. When the man had got away, there had been cries and comments in Arabic, but now there was complete silence. It was as if every man had stopped dead in his tracks at a given signal.

The noise had been heard in the other offices too, and Lambert found himself crossing the street at the same time as his brother, who went straight to the man on the ground and bent over him. His shirt was stained with blood. His eyes were staring upwards. He did not utter a single moan.

'What happened, Oscar?'

'It happened so fast that I hardly saw anything. They were on the planks, one behind the other, each carrying his load, and the one in front was talking in a low voice. I noticed it. They didn't seem to be arguing. It looked instead as if the first one were saying a prayer. The picture changed in a flash, and I didn't have time to move. The one behind dropped his load of bricks on the dock, pulled out a knife from under his shirt, threw himself on the other one, and stabbed him in the back.'

Marcel, who was still kneeling beside the wounded man, was giving orders to one of the clerks who had followed him. Other employees stepped out of the office hesitantly. The typists were standing at the windows.

'That's about all. Two of the men grabbed the fellow with the knife and all the others started talking at the same time in their lingo. I think they were ordering them to let go. If they tried to hold him back, they didn't try very hard, and in order to catch him now . . .'

'Who is he?'

'Mohammed something-or-other. I've got the name on my list.'

The clerk came back with a first-aid kit, which was often needed in the plant. Marcel was in his element. He was calm and meticulous and kept giving brief instructions to his assistant in the manner of a surgeon.

'Serious?'

'I don't think so.'

The Arab was watching them as tranquilly as if he had nothing to do with what was going on, and the others remained standing in a silent circle.

'Has anyone sent for the police?' asked Lambert.

'I've contacted Benezech,' replied Marcel.

The siren of the commissioner's car pierced the air, and a few moments later Benezech arrived.

'A fight?' he asked as he shook Lambert's hand.

'We don't know. They were unloading bricks when the man who was behind this one suddenly went for him and stabbed him.'

'Is he an Arab too?'

'Yes.'

'Did they let him get away?'

'Two of them tried to hold him back, but . . .´

'Hell!'

Benezech turned to Oscar.

'Do you have their names and addresses?'

'I've got the list in the plant.'

'Go and get it.'

The Police Chief stood looking at the man who was stretched out on the gravel.

'I suppose you don't have anything to say?'

The North African's face remained motionless. He merely stared at Benezech with expressionless eyes.

'You don't know anything, do you? Neither why he stabbed you nor . . .'

He shrugged and turned to an inspector.

'Send for an ambulance and have him taken to the hospital.'

He stepped aside to talk to Oscar, who had brought the list. Edmonde was also at a window. Her black dress made her skin seem whiter. But she was not facing the group on the dock. Following the direction of her gaze, Lambert caught sight of the man with the goats who was standing near a tree, about twenty yards away.

Some cars had stopped and a few passers-by had gathered, with the result that Lambert had not seen him.

He was not dressed up as he had been the day before, but was wearing his everyday clothes. He stood there, tall and gaunt, leaning against the trunk of the tree and idly plucking the leaves of a small branch he had picked up from the ground. He was not interested in the wounded Arab, but in Lambert, who thought he could see the glee in the man's pale grey eyes.

Now that he had come back, it was no longer possible to think that his stroll along the quay the day before was merely a matter of chance, and now, because of Benezech's presence, the menace was more definite than ever. The Chief of Police, who was still in conversation with Oscar and taking notes, had his back to the man, but a minute or two later, when the siren of the ambulance was heard, he turned around.

Then—Lambert was sure of it—Benezech's gaze, which had not been fixed on anything in particular, spotted the unexpected figure of the man with the goats, returned to it a second later, this time with a quizzical expression, and lingered on it for some moments.

It was more subtle than that, swifter. Lambert nonetheless caught the look of surprise that flashed across Benezech's face. The commissioner knew the man and did not expect to find him on the Quai Colbert.

It was almost over. Benezech was talking to the attendants, who had brought a stretcher. Marcel, who was now standing up, was informing them of what he had just been doing for the victim, while Oscar was trying to gather his men in order to send them back to work.

The faces were no longer at the windows. Slowly, with animal-like movements, as if not to attract attention, the man with the goats moved off between the lines of perspective of the trees, but Lambert had time to catch his eye before he disappeared.

One of the attendants shut the doors of the ambulance, and the vehicle drove off. Marcel, Benezech, and an inspector formed a group in the sunlight in front of one of the pyramids of bricks. Lambert spotted the little girl from the barge, who had been on deck all the time watching what was going on.

'We'll find him,' Benezech was saying. 'We'll get our hands on him sooner or later. But in spite of what we do we won't learn a thing, and it'll be a devil of a job getting any of the others to testify against him. The victim himself won't say anything.'

Was it an illusion or was he now really looking at Lambert somewhat the way he had looked at the man with the goats a few minutes before, as if a thought had just occurred to him?

'Which of you saw the incident?'

'Oscar.'

'Did you, Lambert?'

'I ran to the window as soon as I heard the noise, but the victim was already on the ground and the other fellow broke away and started running.'

'And you?'

It was Marcel's turn.

'I saw even less than that. A man running, a man on the ground, and the others watching.'

The man with the goats, like the fugitive, must have gone through the alley, which was formed by garden walls on one side and a fence on the other and which led to the Rue des Capucines. It was one of the quietest and most deserted spots in town. The foliage of the trees overflowed the walls of the monastery, and there was only one small door which nobody ever used.

'I'm obliged to send for all these fellows in order to question them. Do you need them long?'

'The unloading should be over tomorrow afternoon.'

'Then I'll get them to come Wednesday morning.'

He shook hands with Marcel and then with Lambert.

'Bridge this evening?'

'Probably.'

Did he look at him differently from the way he usually did, quizzically, with a puzzled expression?

Lambert crossed the street again and went through the big office where he passed Edmonde, who was filing letters. When he was alone, he was seized with anguish and almost called her. What he was now afraid of was not the threat, which was still indefinite, that hung over him, but the possibility of being refused the joy he had promised himself that morning.

In his voluptuous torpor, lying against Léa's warm, soft body, he had envisaged the scene down to the most minute details, some of which were impossible. In broad daylight he had had to give up some of his dreams.

There was nothing to prevent him from calling her right away and shutting the door, or from driving off with her anywhere.

What kept him from doing it? He didn't know. It seemed to him that the time wasn't ripe. He wanted it to be so extraordinary this time that he had a kind of stage-fright and put it off till later. Besides, hadn't he given her to understand earlier that it would be in the afternoon?

He wanted to brood over his desire, to make it so acute, so painful, that the appeasing of it would send him out of this world.

The telephone rang as he was about to leave. It was Nicole, who was calling from the flat, where she was probably tidying up.

'Has there been a fight?' she asked.

'A stabbing.'

'Anyone killed?'

'No. Marcel thinks it's not a serious wound.'

'Are you going out?'

'I'm going to the Renondeau farm.'

141

'Watch out.'

He was struck by the words. It was the second time that day that he had been given a kind of warning, as if there were a fateful sign on his forehead. Léa had said to him dreamily, as she stood naked in the doorway, '*Watch out for yourself.*'

His wife had merely said, '*Watch out.*'

It was vaguer. It could mean drive carefully. She knew he had been drinking the night before and probably supposed that he wasn't quite himself.

'See you later,' he answered.

And the next moment, as he walked across the big office, he looked at Edmonde with such intensity that the expression on his face must have been dramatic.

Neither of them said anything. She seemed to him even more inscrutable than usual, but he felt sure that there was a promise in her eyes.

Neither of them was cheerful. They were never cheerful. Wasn't there now something of the outcast about them? Nevertheless, Lambert was convinced of their own innocence. He would have liked to proclaim it to the world, but without hope of being heard.

By Benezech less than anyone else. Benezech, who, according to what Léa had told him, had trembled with desire in the girl's presence and who, when she had offered herself, had resisted coyly and consoled himself with a poor joke.

'*Maybe in a few years, when I retire . . .*'

Léa had admired him! Léa was fond of him, she respected him.

She had said to Lambert, without knowing anything, '*Watch out for yourself.*'

He was on his way down the short staircase leading to

the yard when he heard his brother's voice behind him:

'One moment, Joseph!'

He waited. Marcel arrived. His lips were quivering.

'I have just one thing to say. When you're back in your normal state, I'd like you to apologize in front of my clerks. There are limits. That's all.'

He shot back:

'My answer is no.'

Marcel was standing a step above Joseph. They stared at each other, then turned their backs without another word.

He would not apologize, either to Marcel or anyone else, because he owed no apologies to anyone, because he wasn't guilty of anything, whatever he might have thought earlier. He was sure he wasn't and he felt more and more convinced every minute.

It was so true, in fact, that he had no particular feeling about taking the road to Château Roisin and even felt completely indifferent when, a short way before the Despujol's grocery-café, he passed the man with the goats who was striding along the road. His goats, which were higher up along the Big Hill, in a tiny meadow surrounded by barbed wire, were bleating for him because they were troubled by his absence.

Renondeau was in the midst of gathering the second crop.

'Did you meet them?' he asked, wiping his face with his sleeve and putting out his calloused hand.

'The gendarmes. Not ours, those from Marpou. They must have gone farther up to see old Jouanneau. It's at least the third time I've been asked the same questions. They're doing the same thing at every farm. First the gendarmes from here, who are friends, then the men from

143

police headquarters, now the gendarmes from Marpou: "What were you doing on Wednesday between five and six o'clock, where were you standing, could you see the cars on the road, did you notice a Citroën?"'

'What did you answer?'

'The truth, of course!'

Had Renondeau informed them that Lambert had left his farm and driven in the direction of the Big Hill twenty minutes before the accident and that there had been a woman in his car?

He dared not ask.

'Well, what about the concrete?' asked the farmer. 'Shall we take a look?'

They went to see the foreman. Before leaving, Lambert was invited to have the traditional glass of white wine in the shed.

'You're a hell of a lucky man, Monsieur Lambert.'

'Why?'

'In the first place, because you make money hand over fist without having to pitch in. And then, because you're always driving around all over the region and because you have every possible opportunity. I, for one, would give a lot to say a word or two to the young lady who was with you the other day. . . .'

It was odd that he felt that way about Edmonde. In the office, for example, she was far from being appreciated by the men. Could it be that the farmer had caught on just by looking at her?

'Here's to your health and hers!'

'Here's to yours, Renondeau.'

'Just between the two of us, when you're in the meadow down below, don't feel shy!'

He winked. One day in June when Lambert had

stopped with Edmonde behind a hedge, he had not realized that he was on Renondeau's land. It was not the time when they heard a noise, but, as he now saw, the peasant nevertheless had his eyes open.

'No harm done, I hope?'

'None at all.'

It was the farmer who blushed.

'A terrific female!' he sighed.

When Lambert got into his car, he regretted not having taken her along. There was no waggon on the road that day, nobody in sight, and he glanced anxiously at the spot where she had jumped across the ditch the last time.

It was too late to go and get her. The whistle would be blowing at the plant in a few minutes, and the employees would all be knocking off for lunch.

He had made up his mind that he would question her afterwards, when his waking dream was fulfilled.

Would she answer? Did she realize how far they had both gone? They were not lovers like other people, they were not lovers at all, they were and had always been two accomplices.

What he wanted to know, and he would make her tell him, was whether she felt guilty. He was sure she didn't. If she had felt guilty, she wouldn't have been what she was. But he felt the need to hear it from her own mouth. He would do anything for that, he would hurt her until she spoke.

Because he had been content merely to follow her, to find in her what he had been groping for all his life.

The others didn't count. With them, even with Léa, he had merely performed obscene movements that left no trace.

145

The revelation he had had of their power to flee . . .

Two gendarmes who were standing near a small black car signalled to him to stop. One of them put his hand to his cap and went up to him.

'Are you from round here?'

They must have been from Marpou, for he didn't know them and they didn't know him either.

'Joseph Lambert,' he said, 'the contractor on the Quai Colbert.'

He handed them his driver's licence and registration card, and the gendarme took notes in his little book.

'I wasn't driving too fast, was I?'

'No. We have orders to stop all Citroëns. Do you have business around here?'

'I'm doing a job at the Renondeau farm.'

'Do you go there often?'

'Almost every day at the present time, to check on how the work is going.'

'Were you there Wednesday afternoon?'

'I was.'

'Around what time?'

'I must have got there around four-thirty and left at about five. I didn't look at my watch.'

'Did you go by way of the Big Hill?'

He hesitated, his mouth was dry.

'I did.'

'Before the accident?'

'I suppose so, since I didn't see anything.'

'Did you go straight back to town?'

'I stopped at the Tréfoux dairy farm, where I have another job going.'

It was already over. The gendarme handed back his papers and again touched his cap.

146

'You're the tenth one this morning,' he said, as if to comfort him.

Lambert returned his salute. The gendarme was not aware of anything, but the information would sooner or later end up somewhere, perhaps on Benezech's desk, where it would be examined in the light of other facts.

'*Watch out for yourself*,' Léa had advised him.

'*Watch out*,' Nicole had said to him on the telephone.

Edmonde had merely looked into his eyes with an expression that had meaning only for him and her.

The man with the goats was beginning to walk up the Big Hill with his usual long strides and recognized him. Their gazes met. Again there was that look of diabolical joy in the man's eyes.

Chapter Eight

HIS only fear, in the beginning, was that they might come for him before Edmonde got back. As for the rest of it, he had stopped hoping. Actually, he had known from the very first day that his life would never be the same again, that the Château Roisin accident had cut it in two. If he had struggled, it was because his nature forced him to fight against men and fate.

It was now only a question of hours or minutes. All that mattered was the appointment he had made with himself as much as, and perhaps more than, with Edmonde.

As for the rest, he no longer cared. At lunch, alone with Nicole, he looked at the flat around him as if it were a strange setting and at his wife as if she were someone who had nothing in common with him. Their years together had left no mark. Nothing remained between them, not even, for example, the familiarity that exists between men who have shared the same barrack room.

It was as if she knew, as if she had been warned by some instinct, she who was so mistrustful of instincts. She spoke in a more subdued, more neutral tone, with a certain softness in her manner, as one speaks to a sick person or to someone who is going away forever.

He was not excited, but simply anxious. He was thinking not about Nicole, but about Edmonde, about the minutes separating him from her return.

The other fear did not come over him until later, when he went downstairs and strolled about, first in the offices and then in the plant and stockrooms where work had started again, and this fear was even less rational than the first.

What if Edmonde didn't come? What if there were a hitch? What if someone, for some unforeseeable reason, detained her elsewhere? That had never happened. She was punctual. In over a year, she had never taken sick leave. He seemed to be trying to find reasons for torturing himself. Every time he looked at his wrist-watch, his impatience increased. At ten minutes to two, he was already standing on the pavement near the Citroën.

Marcel arrived and got out of his car. He looked at his brother with a scowl but did not say a word.

Lambert no longer cared what anyone might think of him, particularly Marcel. He no longer had time to bother about others. He had something to do, and it had become an obsession, an obsession that was now emptied of all he had put into it that morning as he lay half-awake.

Even if it was to be only a kind of symbol, it was essential that it exist. The rest had receded into the background, had faded away. The employees were returning from lunch, and he looked at them as if he had never seen them before.

When she rounded the corner of the Rue de la Ferme in her black dress and white hat, he opened the door much too soon and stood there motionless, no doubt absurd-looking, waiting for her. He motioned to her not to go to the office but to join him.

Somewhat confused, she obeyed and sat down in the front seat, with her handbag, which was as white as her hat, on her knees.

He kept himself from sighing 'At last'.

Without looking at her, as if he were making off with stolen goods, he brutally started the engine and threw in the clutch, and he drove off so noisily that two or three faces appeared at the windows.

'I was afraid,' he said, unable to refrain from admitting it.

'Of what?'

The time for self-respect was over.

'That you weren't coming.'

He still did not look at her and did not see her reaction. She said nothing. Was she surprised? Did she understand him? Or was his image of Edmonde a figment of his imagination?

Could it be, as the young mason had crudely put it, that she was only an *animal*?

He drove fast, cut corners. When he reached the open road, he looked in the mirror to make sure that no car was following him.

He had won! He was proud, happy, as if he had just gained a major victory. On the main road he stepped on the gas in order to relax and at the same time blew his horn. It sounded like a cry of triumph. He drove through villages, along broad stretches of flat meadows. Edmonde was as motionless as ever. She looked straight ahead. He could not yet tell whether she was in unison with him, whether she realized that today it had to be ten times, a hundred times more wonderful than ever before. He turned left at a crossroad and shot forward. Orville Forest, where he had a permit to shoot and where he went from time to time, was not far off, beyond a former forester's lodge which had been transformed into an inn that was frequented by shooting parties. About half a mile away was a road that cut through the forest. He was planning

150

to leave the car at the side of the road and go off with Edmonde to the woods.

'What's the matter?'

He had just sworn angrily at the sight of two men carrying rifles who were leaving the restaurant followed by their dogs. He knew both of them. One was Weisberg, the other Jean Rupert, who ran a sweet shop in the Rue Saint-Martin. He hadn't realized that it was a Monday, that most of the stores in town were closed, and that it was the shopkeepers' day off. Weisberg, who had recognized him, waved at him.

It was now impossible to take the road he had planned to take because the two men would be coming along soon. The whole forest was closed to him, for others were probably out shooting too.

He had frowned, his eyes had grown hard. At the next crossing, he took the sunken road that went downhill. He was forced to change his plans, to improvise. At the foot of the hill was a pond, known as Notre Dame Pond, which was surrounded by a few trees. It was too muddy for fishing and the shore was usually deserted.

Edmonde sat quietly while he drove, glancing at him occasionally with a puzzled expression. She must have sensed his tension, which had been heightened by the obstacles. She was not anxious but only surprised.

With a menacing look, he stopped the car at the side of the road, in the mud.

'Get out,' he ordered and then slammed the door.

They had only a hundred yards to walk along the path in order to reach the water, but they did not go to the end of it, for they suddenly heard the yells of children and then saw half a dozen local boys bathing nude in the pond.

151

He was grateful to her for not smiling, for awaiting his decision without looking him in the face. The very excessiveness of his disappointment restored his calm.

'Come! I apologize.'

The other places which he knew were not in that direction but on the other side of town, along the canal or on the way to the Renondeau farm. He didn't want to run the risk of showing his face in the streets, and so the only thing left was to look around for some deserted spot.

He was clinging to his desire. As he stepped into the car, he feverishly lit a cigarette and muttered, 'It's idiotic!'

He was aware of the absurdity of the situation but was unable to laugh at it. On the contrary, for him it was the threat of a death-blow, of a grotesque end. It brought to mind the silent laughter of the man with the goats, and he was sorry he hadn't gone to see him the night before and got the thing over with, as he had thought of doing for a moment.

He avoided looking at Edmonde lest he realize that the girl at his side was an ordinary typist who wanted to get back to the peaceful, reassuring setting of the office as quickly as possible.

It wasn't true! He recalled ineffable details which would probably have meant little to anyone else but which meant a lot to him—for example, the time when she was lying on her back and staring, as if fascinated, at the sturdy trunk of an oak tree. He had understood that fascination because of the way she had just reacted. For her, the mighty tree was another principle of life, like the male organ that she was caressing, and when she saw sap flowing from the wound of a pine tree she naturally thought of a man's sap. In her mind, everything merged, everything that swells with life, everything that reproduces, everything that tends obscurely towards natural fullness.

He had stopped once again at the side of the road and now sat at the wheel with a vacant expression. She looked at him in surprise.

He merely tossed away his half-smoked cigarette.

'Let's go!' he sighed.

He had just wavered. His faith was now less firm. He doubted. He had been on the point of suddenly turning around and going back to town without trying the experiment. He drove slowly, almost relaxed, as if it were now less important, looking at the roads that came into view, in search of a lonely spot as if they were stupid Sunday lovers.

Two or three times, he thought he had found one, but there was a jinx on him. Each time, at the last moment, he caught sight of a peasant in his field, an old woman looking after her cow, a nearby house that he hadn't seen at first.

He no longer knew where he was, for he had kept away from the main roads and had been going round in circles. He ended by following, without much hope, a bumpy road that suddenly ended in the middle of nowhere. Two fences opened out on meadows where black and white cows were grazing. Nearby were thorny hedges where the grass was thick and dark green. The damp ground was shaded by three big elms.

Realizing that this was the place, she got out of the car with him. For the first time, each was as embarrassed as the other. He would have liked to talk before they went any further. Earlier, while waiting for her on the pavement of the Quai Colbert, he had planned to talk about himself and had even prepared whole sentences. Like his

153

dreams that morning, they were no longer in keeping with reality. They had become meaningless, they would have rung false.

He walked to the second fence and saw that there were cows in both meadows. At the far end of the one on the right, above the line of the horizon, he made out the red roof of a farm.

'Lie down,' he said in a hoarse tone.

She hesitated a moment, then sat down in the grass, ten feet away from the muddy car.

'Lie down!' he repeated, kneeling beside her.

He had to. He had promised himself. It was a test. He owed it to himself to go through with it.

'Lift up your dress.'

He stared at her face, which was turned upwards. He wanted it to be as it had been the other times, better than the others, and suddenly, with a rough movement, he uncovered her belly and threw himself on it in a fury.

She had not moved. She was not afraid. But the pupils of her eyes, which were still gazing upwards, had become more set, and her mouth had quivered with pain.

'Do you understand?' he growled, mindless of what he was saying, for there was no relationship between his thoughts and words.

He was relentless, almost fierce, and watched her face cruelly.

'Tell me, do you understand? You've got to understand. Do you hear? I've got to know . . .'

Three times he hoped. Three times he thought he was going to triumph, for her nostrils dilated and her upper lip began to draw back with the expression that haunted him, that he had to see again at any cost because it was the sign.

154

It was essential that it happen again, for it would prove that he was right, that it was on the Big Hill, when the bus had screamed, that he had been wrong.

'Do you understand, tell me? Do you understand?'

Then, just as he was about to reach the goal, her features lost their tension, a salty teardrop oozed from her eyelid, only one, and she dropped her limp arms and moaned in a low voice, 'I can't. Forgive me.'

His body slackened, and he stood up. He avoided looking at her while she in turn got to her feet and arranged her dress. He heard her walk to the car, where she remained standing in front of the door, waiting for him with her head bowed.

When he finally went to the car, he was himself again, or seemed to be, but his features were drawn and his eyes had a vacant look.

'Are you angry with me?' she murmured.

He shook his head, took his seat, and started the engine.

She must have believed him, must have thought it didn't matter, for her face had taken on the serene expression it had in the office.

They had nothing to say to each other. Since he was unable to turn the car around, he drove in reverse. After two bends in the road, he was back on the main road. He hadn't realized it was so near.

What she would probably never suspect was that a few minutes before, when she had been looking up at the white clouds in the sky, he had resisted a desire to destroy her.

It was over. He was now so calm that she was surprised and from time to time stole a glance at him. He seemed to be smiling. Perhaps he really was. The grimace of the man with the goats was also a smile. It no longer mattered. Nothing mattered now. If he had been mistaken, that

155

concerned no one but him, and it didn't mean he was entirely wrong.

Could it be that when the tear of impotence had flowed from her eye she was thinking of the bus that had screamed with fear behind them, or of the still joyful faces of the children who were going to burn?

He had thought of them, too.

What about it? Did that prove they were guilty? Had she felt guilty, had she felt ashamed?

That too was of no importance. The girl sitting beside him was Mademoiselle Pampin, and he had nothing in common with Mademoiselle Pampin, apart from dictating letters and other office routine. No letters today. Nor was there any need to take her to any of the plants.

He was almost embarrassed by her presence, the presence he had longed for so eagerly. She had become even more foreign to him than Nicole. The image of her and her mother, arm in arm, walking in the Town Hall Square, flashed across his mind and seemed grotesque.

He was really smiling, but she wasn't the kind of person who could have interpreted that smile. Perhaps the man with the goats?

As they neared town, the setting became more familiar. He looked without seeing at villages, at châteaux, at a bridge over a river, sights on which his eyes had rested thousands of times.

There was now no reason to hurry, nor was there any need, as when he drove down the Big Hill, to go slowly.

What sign had Nicole and Léa seen on his face? It puzzled him. He was sure that something was eluding him.

'*Watch out for yourself,*' Léa had said, she who, a moment before, had so nicely spread her thighs and whom he had disdained.

156

'*Watch out*,' his wife had cautioned him on the telephone.

He crossed the bridge over the canal where, as a child, he had caught his first fish with a stick, a piece of string, and a bent pin. In front of him, on the white wall, he could see the words:

'*J. Lambert & Sons*'.

The North Africans were still walking up the springy planks to the barge and coming down in Indian file laden with bricks.

He stopped the car at the kerb and opened the door for Edmonde, who, without waiting for him, walked towards the office.

The last thing he looked at on the dock was the pink bow in the hair of the little girl from the barge.

Then he in turn went up the six stairs and opened the door. Mademoiselle Berthe, one of the clerks who acted as telephone operator, a chubby little woman with a dimpled chin, said to him, 'Monsieur Benezech telephoned. He asked you to ring him as soon as you get back.'

'I know,' he replied absently.

'Shall I put the call through?'

'In a little while.'

Edmonde, who was already seated at her varnished table, was taking out her pencils and erasers. Marcel was watching him through the glass wall of the draughtsmen's office.

Lambert turned around to look at Monsieur Bicard in his cubbyhole. The yellow can of catechu was next to the big account book.

He opened the door of his office, hesitated, then closed it behind him. The windows were open, and the smell of pitch reached him from the barge.

Because of the bricks which the men had been unloading for three days, specks of pink dust were dancing in the sunlight. He sat down at his desk, calmly. As he opened the pad to take a sheet of paper, he thought of his brother Fernand, whom he knew so little. There was no time to waste, for anyone might drop in and he hadn't wanted to bolt the door.

With the blue pencil that he used for annotating documents, he printed the words:

'*I am not guilty*'.

He laid the sheet on the blotter, opened the right-hand drawer, and pulled out the army revolver that he had brought back from the war. No longer remembering whether it was loaded, he had to make sure.

He granted himself another moment to look out of the window. His eyes sought the pink ribbon in the hair of the little girl.

He did not see her. It was four o'clock and she had probably gone to the cabin for her afternoon snack.

He glanced at the ceiling, wondering whether his wife was upstairs. Then, very quickly, he had a vision of what would happen in a few moments, the coming and going, the panic, the phone calls, the sudden stopping of work in the office and the plant.

He also thought of the burial, of the family group, including little Motard and his son-in-law, of the other groups, the office staff, his friends, his cronies at the Café Riche, the shooting club, the clients, the suppliers, the anonymous crowd.

Last, he thought of Léa, but he refused to think of Edmonde.

He started to raise the barrel of the revolver to his mouth, knowing that the thing to do was to fire into the mouth, upwards, but he paused and laid the weapon on the desk. His eyes were staring at the sheet of paper.

He again picked up the big blue pencil, then hesitated, pensively, as to whether to cross out what he had written or correct it. Finally, changing his mind again, he crumpled the sheet in his hand and threw it into the waste-paper basket.

What was the use? Was it for him to decide?

He had the impression that footsteps were approaching, that someone was going to knock at the door, and, shutting his eyes, he hurriedly fired.